D0838291

Blaze™

Dear Reader,

I love connected stories—reading them, and writing them, too! I'm excited to introduce connected stories with this month's release, *Making a Splash* and next month's *Riding the Storm*. What made it even more fun for me was writing them for The Wrong Bed miniseries, which many readers already know is a perennial favorite of mine! Now, I have the unique pleasure of visiting The Wrong Bed: Again and Again, with two stories where a couple of hero brothers trade boats for a week.

My first hero, Jack Murphy, has no idea that there's a surprise waiting for him belowdecks when he boards his brother's power catamaran. But his brother set him up precisely so he'd have no choice but to face the One That Got Away, sexy water sports instructor Alicia LeBlanc. Keith is pretty pleased with himself, but cosmic payback is inevitable next month in *Riding the Storm!*

I hope you enjoy visiting The Wrong Bed, too! Thanks so much for reading and don't forget to check out my website at www.joannerock.com for a contest every month to win free books and more.

Happy Reading,

Joanne Rock

Joanne Rock

MAKING A SPLASH

TORONTO NEW YORK LONDON
AMSTERDAM PARIS SYDNEY HAMBURG
STOCKHOLM ATHENS TOKYO MILAN MADRID
PRAGUE WARSAW BUDAPEST AUCKLAND

Recycling programs
for this product may
not exist in your area.

ISBN-13: 978-0-373-79640-3

MAKING A SPLASH

Copyright © 2011 by Joanne Rock

ABOUT THE AUTHOR

The mother of three sports-minded sons, Joanne Rock's primary occupation is carting kids to practices and cheering on their athletic prowess at any number of sporting events. In the windows of time between football games, she loves to write and cheer on happily-ever-afters. A three-time RITA® Award nominee, Joanne is the author of more than fifty books for a variety of Harlequin series. She has been an *RT Book Reviews* Career Achievement nominee and multiple Reviewers' Choice finalist, including a nomination for *The Captive* (Blaze #534) as Best Blaze of 2010. Her work has been reprinted in twenty-six countries and translated into nineteen languages. Over two million copies of her books are in print. For more information on Joanne's books, visit www.joannerock.com.

Books by Joanne Rock

To my sister and brother-in-law,
Linda and Bob Watson.
Thank you for letting me hang out on the boat
and for giving me another book idea. Turns out
my Florida visits are not only fun and fattening
but creatively productive, as well. I appreciate you!

Prologue

JACK MURPHY HAD BEEN BACK in town for less than four weeks since he'd completed his navy contract and returned to Chatham, Massachusetts, from Bahrain. Already Keith had noted the changes in his older brother. Jack was quieter. More brooding than he used to be. And he refused to resume his old job as VP of global properties for Murphy Resorts, the family business.

Perhaps most notably, he hadn't bothered to show up for a family football game the day before, even though all the Murphy brothers were back in town at once—something that hadn't happened since Christmas three years ago. Clearly, something was wrong.

Keith watched him now as they shared a table at their oldest brother's engagement party on the lawn of the family's home overlooking the Atlantic Ocean. Jack stared out at the waves, while one table over their father tapped his beer bottle to signal for the crowd's attention.

There were six brothers—five by birth plus Axel, the foster brother from Finland who'd been with them for eight years. Out of the six of them, Jack and Keith had both landed in the middle, with twenty-eight-year-old Jack eleven months older than Keith. They shared a look—the family pictures proved it (as well as the face that Keith dressed better than the rest). All the brothers had inherited their father's green eyes, in varying shades, and dark brown hair. Even Axel fit the mold, except for his blue eyes. Danny and Kyle—twenty-six and twenty-five years old respectively—carried the most muscle. Jack was the tallest. The other differences were in the way they carried themselves. Ryan was the corporate shark who would take over the family business. Jack was ex-Navy, clean-cut and brooding. Keith the GQ charmer—he'd like to think—who'd developed his own company. Danny was a former rocker with a goatee and bad-ass sneer, but he'd joined the Navy, too, and had no plans to get out. Kyle was a hockey superstar whose nose had taken its fair share of hits. Axel had come to the U.S. to ease his transition into the National Hockey League after playing on college teams with Kyle.

As the family peacemaker, Keith naturally felt compelled to pinpoint the problem with Jack. He'd ruled out post-traumatic stress disorder last week, thank God, after strong-arming his closemouthed brother into talking about his second overseas stint in four years. Instead of PTSD, he'd discovered that Jack had a woman problem.

And that, Keith planned to address tonight.

"To the future bride and groom!" Their father's hearty toast reverberated through the huge outdoor tent on the lawn.

On cue, Keith clanked glasses with his brothers in honor of Ryan and his bride to be. At least *one* of the Murphy men was in a good mood today.

Not that they weren't all glad for Ryan, whose hard work with Murphy Resorts had more than earned him some personal happiness. That's why all the Murphys had heeded the call to return to the sprawling house on Cape Cod for tonight's brouhaha.

Jack didn't bother suppressing a scowl despite the festivities. Even as the chamber ensemble gave way to a lively dance band that cranked up tunes for the future bride and groom, Jack slid back into his chair after the toast and drummed his fingers on the white linen tablecloth.

The guy's problem had a name, of course. Alicia LeBlanc. She was a firecracker and just the kind of woman a strong-willed man needed. But with two ardent opinions at work, they'd been too stubborn to see the possibilities of a future together, and Jack had joined the navy at a critical juncture in their relationship, telling her not to wait for him.

Nothing like slamming a door on a future.

The family had assumed four years away from home—returning only on the occasional leave—would cure Jack of Alicia. But he'd come back from Bahrain more restless and edgy than ever. Something needed to be settled between those two, one way or another.

Luckily, Keith had a plan to shove his hardheaded brother in the right direction—he just happened to have the woman in question aboard his boat and docked nearby at this very moment. Because of his success starting up the environmental consulting firm he now ran, Alicia had approached Keith two weeks ago with some questions about developing a business plan for a bed-and-breakfast she hoped to purchase. He might have simply given her the advice and sent her on her way. But the inn she wanted was up in Bar Harbor, Maine, close to where Keith was headed. He needed to hand off the catamaran to one of his company's VIPs as part of a corporate incentives reward. He'd agreed to give Alicia all the help she wanted, but because of his busy schedule, he'd talked her into discussing her plans on the ride to Bar Harbor. It would save him time, and allow her to view the property.

They were supposed to leave right after Ryan's engagement party. Right after Keith trotted out a little old-fashioned maneuvering to make sure Jack was aboard the catamaran for the trip north tonight instead of him.

"So how's the *Vesta* handling these days?" Keith began, turning the discussion to watercraft as the band launched into "Moonglow" and their parents took the floor beneath a small chandelier suspended under one of the tent canopies. "Are you getting tired of sailing solo yet?"

It was a comfortable, easy place to begin a familiar

argument about the merits of their respective boats, and Keith tipped back the last of his champagne while he watched Jack's scowl deepen. Around the small table, Danny peeled the label on his microbrew while Kyle thumbed a text message faster than a teenage girl in spite of his massive hands. Axel furtively checked his PDA for rival-team hockey scores. The mild evening weather stirred a breeze fragrant with late blooming flowers the landscaper had imported for the occasion.

"She's as smooth as ever," he muttered, although he didn't rise to defend the twenty-six-foot vintage fiber-glass sailboat with the same fire as usual. "But I've got an offer on her and I'm taking her down to Charleston this week to meet with a potential buyer."

Crap.

Keith hadn't planned for that possibility, thinking he could goad Jack into a boat switch for a few days with no problem.

"You're selling the *Vesta?*" This surprised him for a few reasons, not the least of which was because the *Vesta* was the first sailboat he'd ever purchased, and he'd christened it with Alicia.

What if Jack was truly making an effort to move on?

"Probably. Maybe." He shrugged. "Heading south this time of year is bound to be a good idea either way. I'm doing some investing in local businesses and figured I might as well free up my capital to continue in that direction."

What direction? Keith wanted to shout, since invest-ing hardly amounted to the kind of hands-on work Jack preferred. His brother really did need help finding his way back to a satisfying civilian life.

All the more reason for Keith to forge ahead with his plan, right?

"Yeah?" Thinking fast, he tried to figure out how to make the scheme come together in light of the new wrinkle. "You ought to let me deliver the *Vesta* for you, bro. I have a client I need to see down that way and I'm well overdue for some time off."

Jack snorted. "You? Sail the *Vesta* solo all the way to South Carolina?" He shook his head. "You forget, a vintage classic like a Pearson Triton doesn't come equipped with all the techno-gadgets you need on the miniature corporate yacht you've got. I don't know how you'd manage without satellite positioning and automatic docking."

"Is that right?" Keith felt the same thrill as when he had a new client on the line, ready to close a deal that would reap fat rewards for his growing business. He could tell he had Jack on the hook. "I'll bet I could handle the *Vesta* a whole hell of a lot easier than you could navigate a state-of-the-art, forty-five-foot power catamaran on your own."

Across the table, Daniel's eyes flicked their way and Kyle set down his BlackBerry, the brothers drawn into the bickering like moths to a flame. Hell, they'd forged a brotherhood by more than blood—which was why super-competitive Axel had fit right in. Every Murphy present was used to the unspoken family code of "don't talk the talk if you can't walk the walk."

And they all talked a damned good game. Bets and competitions were their way of life. No clan affair was complete without an impromptu game of football or a wager over who could throw a ball, horseshoe, javelin, you-name-it the farthest.

"Do you remember who you're talking to?" Jack shook his head in disbelief, though he lowered his voice in deference to the fact that their mother had zeroed in on their table and was making her way toward them with determined steps. "You think I don't know state-of-the-art boats? I've been in the U.S. *Navy* for the last four years."

The hard glint in Jack's eyes told Keith his brother wasn't backing down. Of course Jack could handle the boat. It was Alicia LeBlanc who would provide the challenge. And damned if Keith didn't feel the smallest twinge of guilt for sending Jack into the fray unarmed and unaware.

But Keith knew what it was like to get taken in by a manipulative woman. And it pissed him off to think about his brother setting aside someone like Alicia without looking back. People fortunate enough to have something special like that had no business throwing it away.

Their mother arrived at the table in her peach silk dress and dyed-to-match pumps, her outfit perfectly coordinated with the harvest-themed colors of the engagement party. Colleen Murphy was all elegance on the outside with her understated diamond earrings and her French manicure, but she had a steely strength as tough as that of her sons. The fire in her light blue eyes right now suggested her maternal radar had gotten wind of a wager in the making.

"Boys?" She intervened discreetly, her gaze moving over each one slowly. "We agreed there would be no resolving disagreements with feats of strength tonight, remember?"

On cue, Kyle flexed his biceps for show. "As if there was any point to that when the winner is so obvious."

Keith rose to his feet to put her at ease.

"No arguments here, Mom." He kissed her cheek as he pulled a set of keys from his pocket and tossed them on the table. "Jack offered me a chance for a little downtime on the sailboat this week, since I was in the market for a vacation. He offered to take my boat up to Bar Harbor for my company's chief financial officer to use, while I get to sail the *Vesta* down to Charleston to meet a guy who wants to buy it. Just a friendly swap."

Daniel and Axel snickered. Kyle hid his grin behind a champagne glass. And Keith had to pat himself on the back for pulling off this operation so smoothly.

"That's it?" their mother pressed. "A friendly trade?" She peered around the table, daring any of them to disagree.

Jack rose, staring Keith down for a little longer than was strictly necessary before offering a warm smile to their mom.

"That's it," he assured her. He took Keith's keys and pocketed them. "I'm docked two slips down from you, bro. And since I don't have one damn thing worth locking up, you won't need a set of keys to get in. Good luck with a boat that doesn't come with enough horsepower to fuel a jet engine. Sailing single-handed requires elbow grease."

Keith yawned to demonstrate what he thought of the warning. "Not a problem. When you cut yourself off from the rest of the world, it's easy to focus on one thing." He loosened his tie. "I could use the life of leisure for a week."

Keith noticed Kyle whistling under his breath at the implication that Jack was taking it easy. But damn it, when was he going to get back to his position at Murphy Resorts?

Jack seemed ready to fire off a retort when their mom extended a peach-silk-covered arm between them and gestured to Kyle, Axel and Danny.

"Speaking of leisure," she blurted, no doubt to divert them, "there are some lovely young ladies here who would probably enjoy a turn on the dance floor."

How was that for a segue? His brothers took the bait, standing to attend to their bachelor duties as the band began a swing tune.

Jack's jaw flexed in an obvious effort to swallow back whatever he'd been about to say. He tapped Keith in the center of his chest. "Your life is only as complicated as you make it, hotshot. I'll have your boat relocated to Bar Harbor in a few days and leave myself enough time to take in the sights." He turned to their mother and kissed her cheek. "Mom, it's been a pleasure. I'll pay my respects to the happy couple on my way out."

When he had disappeared into the darkness and out of earshot, Colleen peered up at Keith.

"I don't suppose you care to tell me what that was all about?" She twisted the small diamond stud in one ear.

"I'm just trying to remind Jack that ignoring the obstacles in life doesn't make them go away."

"I have no idea what you're talking about and no clue how a week on a spiffed-up catamaran will call to mind any obstacles for Jack." She tipped her head toward his shoulder to murmur a quiet warning. "I hope you know what you're doing."

He thought about Alicia, who should have already arrived aboard his boat and would quite possibly be safely asleep by now, since he'd warned her he would be late. They'd set a tentative time to talk over the business plan tomorrow afternoon. That was his only regret in his scheme to help Jack confront his past: Keith genuinely had some ideas for her. But he'd prepped a file to email her in the morning, so she wouldn't be deprived of that input.

Besides, Jack knew more about the hospitality industry than him after working in the family business. Keith had gotten out from under the family thumb early in his career.

"Trust me." He took his mom's arm and led her toward the dance floor. "When you run as hard and fast as Jack does from happiness, you're bound to slam headfirst into trouble sooner or later. I'm merely speeding up the inevitable collision."

His mother stopped short a few feet shy of the hardwood dance surface. Keith could practically see the wheels turning in her mind, her delicately arched blond brows furrowed in thought before they smoothed out again.

Clearly, she'd reached the logical conclusion about Jack. The one thing he'd run from hard and fast—love, in the form of Alicia LeBlanc.

"Don't tell me Alicia is in Bar Harbor."

"Better yet, she's on my boat." Keith grinned, unrepentant. He tugged his cell phone out of his pocket and slid open the keypad. "But don't worry. I'll give Jack a heads-up…once I'm sure it's too late for him to turn back."

1

JACK'S CELL PHONE buzzed at least three times before he even got his brother's sleek catamaran into open water.

He knew it was nothing pressing, since the text messages had subject lines such as "quick heads-up" rather than "URGENT." So he ignored them, figuring Keith wanted to share a lot of details about his high-end vessel—as if Jack couldn't figure out how to steer a boat without the help of GPS gizmos. Jack had gotten this far in life by knowing when to tune out the rest of the world, a lesson his workaholic brother had yet to process.

Keith the Corporate Mogul took every incoming call as if it were life or death, assuming the world couldn't turn without his input. Jack had weathered enough storms to know plenty of problems blew themselves out without him lifting a finger. While Keith positioned himself for the *Forbes* list, Jack was content to invest some of his savings in local businesses, as he'd been doing since he returned home a month ago. Nothing big. He gave those struggling bars a hand up in a rough economy while he figured out what direction he wanted his career to take now that he was out of the service. Returning to the family business wasn't a direction that particularly appealed.

In the meantime, he'd started selling off a few of his personal possessions to consolidate his assets and simplify his lifestyle. Truth be told, he was glad not to be the one to hand off the vintage Pearson Triton that was full of memories for him. Alicia had helped him christen the *Vesta* back when his life had made more sense.

Not that he would think about her now, damn it. His brother's engagement party had messed with his head tonight, putting thoughts of her back in his brain.

But you broke up with her because she was too young.... Some obnoxious voice in his head piped up. *That problem no longer exists.*

The fact that they'd both matured, however, wouldn't take away their bulldog personalities. Or erase the fact that she'd moved on since he'd been away. Every time he'd been home on leave in the past four years, she'd been dating someone else.

If he had any sense, he would fall for someone softer. Someone who wouldn't argue about his every decision. Someone a whole lot less like him. But first he needed to find a way to come to terms with a shared past he'd never really forgotten.

Now, at about two-thirty in the morning, he had his ropes thrown off and he'd steered through the coastal traffic into open water. He'd checked out the chart plotter and the self-steering feature enough to feel comfortable moving around deck while the boat cruised along. No doubt about it, the catamaran had every cool innovation known to mankind—the Zeus steering system and GPS position-locking features both made handling a big vessel easy.

He figured he'd put enough distance between him and the rest of the Murphy clan to settle down for the night. He was out of the main shipping lanes and his lights were burning bright, so he should be safe to get some rest.

It would kill his mother to know it, but he hated trips home. Being there brought back too many memories of a time where he'd dreamed of a different life.

Jamming the cell phone back in his jacket pocket, he tugged his tie off. The fact that, hours after leaving Ryan's party, Jack hadn't even changed out of his suit yet spoke volumes about his need to be under way, as far from Cape Cod and the possibility of bumping into Alicia as he could get. He needed to see her sooner or later, yes. But not until he figured out why her memory still affected him so strongly.

He'd stopped at a convenience store for some supplies on his way to the marina, despite Keith's assurance that the corporate toy was fully stocked. But other than the one brief pause, he'd been running nonstop since he walked away from the party.

The boat was a beauty. Keith's company owned the power catamaran and used it to entertain clients. But in between gigs to impress potential customers or long-term patrons, the top dogs passed the toy around amongst themselves.

Now that he'd cooled down a bit, he could appreciate some of the features of Keith's catamaran. Roomy as hell. Laid out by someone who'd been at sea before, with no skimping on practical stuff—although there were some fluffy add-ons such as a hot tub in the front deck. Jack switched on the night-light in the hall leading to the forward cabin. He'd done a quick inspection of the hull layout before he'd left the marina, tossing his bag into the cabin that looked as if it had been recently used, with the berth still rumpled and a duffel in one corner. Had to be the space Keith had used, and was therefore the one most likely to have sheets and an alarm clock at the ready.

Yanking off his jacket and belt, Jack trailed clothes like a stripper, too wasted to hang things up. He didn't even bother turning on the light before he slid into the queen-size bed, liking the dark just fine. Oblivion couldn't come soon enough after the day he'd had.

He was happy for Ryan finding The One. Truly, he was. But seeing that promise of a future on both their faces had poured acid in an old wound, reminding Jack of the way Alicia had started to think long-term with him when he'd been embroiled in a family drama that had needed his attention. Those days should have been too long ago for him to remember their breakup in such vivid detail.

Unfortunately, he remembered all too well.

On the plus side, he'd put some serious nautical miles

between himself and the woman he'd walked out on, before he finally drifted into exhausted sleep....

ALICIA LEBLANC COULD almost swear Jack Murphy was back in her arms.

An annoying rational voice—inescapable even in her dreams—told her that was because she was on board a Murphy-owned boat. Dealing with Keith had put his whole family back in the forefront of her mind after all these years, and that's why her subconscious had concocted a delicious nighttime fantasy about her ex.

"Jack..." She sighed his name in her half sleep, resenting the practical side of her that insisted she was just dreaming. Why couldn't she simply enjoy sexy dreams like the rest of the population?

Because dreaming about him makes you weak! her cranky ego shouted.

Undaunted, she pressed her cheek to Jack's broad, bare chest. Her dreams added muscle and weight to his younger body, altering her memories of him to account for the navy-hardened form he sported these days. She'd caught sight of him on the beach earlier in the week, when she'd been giving kite-surfing lessons to tourists—one facet of the water sports business she'd started to save money for her own coastal bed-and-breakfast. Nothing big like Murphy Resorts owned all over the Cape, but something small and personal, where she could entertain all the time and share her love of the water with travelers. She'd been hooking up the safety harness on a couple of college kids who wanted to catch big air on the water when she had heard Jack's voice carrying from farther out in the surf.

Sure enough, he'd sailed into sight on the *Vesta*. She might have taken a moment's pleasure in knowing he'd kept the boat even though he'd dumped her. But he'd probably just been too busy saving the world to ditch the sailboat the second he'd ousted Alicia from his life.

Damn the man.

Still, he was hot and hard everywhere in this dream moment that would be over all too soon. She kissed his chest, her tongue darting along one flat pectoral to steal a taste of him. He was salty with sea air, just the way she remembered. Turning her cheek against him again, she absorbed his warmth, her fingers finding the silky hair at the center of his chest. She followed the path lower, savoring the way his skin tightened at her touch, his muscles twitching in response.

Greedy for more, she rubbed her breasts against him, arching into his body so she touched as much of him as she could. The friction had her heart racing. Pleasure simmered in her veins and she wondered why her brain insisted on maintaining the reality of her tank top between them in the fantasy.

Ditto Jack's boxer shorts.

She'd slid a thigh between his at some point and she resented the presence of lightweight cotton, no matter that the fabric was soft. What she wanted throbbed behind the fly, and she had every intention of enjoying it. Enjoying him.

"Jack," she murmured, liking the feel of his name on her tongue, loving that he felt so real.

Smoothing her fingers over his face, she encountered deep stubble that would sting her cheek if she rubbed it against him there. The strong, square line of his jaw remained as stubborn and immovable as ever, broken only by a dimple centered in his chin. For old time's sake, she touched the depression, but the contact was too full of past emotions when she wanted only passion.

It had been so long for her. No one else compared to this man, even though she'd searched for someone to fill the void in her heart.

But right now, she could have him again.

"Alicia?" His voice warmed her ear, his lips coming alive as she undulated against him.

"Yes," she confirmed, wanting to be the only one he thought about. There'd been a time she'd been certain she was the only woman who mattered to him. "I'm so ready," she whispered, rocking her hips against his.

Heat blossomed between her legs and she palmed his thigh to keep the pressure of him right where she wanted it.

"Alicia." The cold bark of his voice knifed through the dream like a pin to a balloon, deflating all that sexed-up heat.

The warm body beside hers scrambled away. Hell, he scrambled right out of the bed. She blinked in the darkness, her pulse racing as her knee fell against the empty mattress without his thigh to prop hers up. *What the...*

A horrible thought occurred to her.

"I'm not dreaming." She clutched the bedspread to her aching body, straining to see in the cabin with only a sliver of moonlight coming through a porthole and a dull glow from a night-light flickering out in the hall.

She prayed she would wake up, prayed this was a fantasy turned mortifying nightmare. But as she took in Jack Murphy's glowering expression above her, Alicia knew she didn't have enough imagination to conjure up all the fury she saw there.

Oh, God. There must have been some mix-up....

"What are you doing here?" He flipped on an overhead light, frying her retinas and making her all too aware of the thin pajama shorts she'd worn to bed with her tank top.

No, it was Jack's forest-green eyes raking up and down her exposed gams that tripped a keen awareness of the limited wardrobe. Flipping the rest of the bedspread over her lower half, she sat up in the bed.

"I might ask you the same question," she retorted, already imagining ways to strangle Keith for this. "Where is your brother?"

Not waiting for an answer, she hopped off the bed and marched past Jack, ready to duke it out with the only Murphy she'd remained friends with after the big breakup between her and Jack.

"He's not here." Jack halted her forward progress with one long arm, hauling her back into the bedroom. "And if he was, don't you think you're a little underdressed to speak with him?"

The feel of Jack's arm across her stomach, even through double layers of quilt, burned into her skin. Her breast brushed his forearm for the briefest moment, but the memory of that contact remained in her tingling flesh. She tightened her hold on the bedspread, wishing she could squeeze away the sensation.

His naked chest was mere inches from her in the small cabin, the berth just big enough for a bed and a space to dress. It occurred to her she'd actually kissed— licked—that chest only moments ago in her sleep. In fact, her hormones were still so ramped up that the thought of her lips on his tanned skin made her mouth run dry.

"What do you mean, he's not here?" With the lights on and her bare feet planted on the carpeted cabin floor, she realized something was wrong—something beyond finding Jack in her bed. Peering out the nearest port- hole, she couldn't see the marina lights. Dark ocean glimmered back at her. They were out to sea. The be- ginnings of panic tickled the back of her neck. "Where is he?"

"You were waiting for Keith?" Jack ignored her ques- tion to ask his own.

And didn't that help remind her why it was just as well they'd broken up? He was a man accustomed to having his own way.

"Yes, damn it." The panic jumped higher, clogging her throat. "He's supposed to take me to Bar Harbor and help me finalize a business plan on the way. I'm looking at a bed-and-breakfast up there—"

"Why?" Jack interrupted.

That couldn't possibly be jealousy she heard in his voice. Frustration spiked, mingled with embarrassment, and all around made it difficult to maintain her patience.

"First tell me what happened to Keith." She worked up a glower of her own, recalling how Jack could steam-roll her if she didn't give as good as she got with him. "Tell me where we are and why Keith is not here."

She'd save the questions about why Jack felt it was okay to climb into bed with her after breaking her heart and leaving town four years ago. Damn him, she was the one who deserved some answers.

"Keith knew you were on the boat." Jack didn't seem terribly cowed by her threatening glare, but at least he'd paused in the inquisition to take out his cell phone. Tapping some keys, he appeared to scroll through a screen. "That must have been what he texted me about."

"Well, *I* still don't understand." She barreled past him again, determined to check their headings if Jack wouldn't pony up any answers. "Has it occurred to you or your brother that I might have a lot riding on this trip?"

Not waiting for his answers this time, she stomped through the galley and up toward the helm, clutching the spread tight against the sea winds that swirled down the hatch.

"And did you know the Murphys aren't the only people in the world who are passionate about their business?" she asked, on a roll now. "I never would have taken such a slow route to Bar Harbor if Keith hadn't agreed to look over my business plan for me and give me his input on it along the way." An awful thought occurred to her. She whirled around on the stairs to find Jack a half step behind her. "Does this have to do with some brotherly wager?"

Bets and contests of all varieties were favorite pastimes of the Murphy men. Just ask anyone who'd lived in Chatham, Massachusetts, for the last decade. After their family's annual Thanksgiving regatta out on the open water, they returned home for their front-lawn Turkey Bowl, a contest so official there were paid refs imported from out of town. Then there was the bet Jack had once made to see how fast he could talk her into a kiss. Although that one…well, she hadn't been all that offended at the time.

Jack's pause was telling.

"Come back downstairs," he insisted. "We need to talk."

"Hmm. You forget that conversation for you consists of asking all the questions while I do all the answering. Sorry, but I'll pass." She had every intention of reaching Bar Harbor with a workable business plan in place before her appointment with the owner of the seaside bed-and-breakfast she'd had her eye on these last few months. With little capital to put down on the place, she wanted to have a thorough game plan mapped out for the bank. If she couldn't nab a business loan, the inn might wind up in foreclosure.

She needed a fresh start someplace new now that Jack was back home on the Cape. She'd gotten over their breakup a long time ago. Truly, she had. But it had been easier when he was in the navy and she didn't have to see him around town. Now that he'd started investing in businesses around Chatham—a fact well circulated by the local rumor mill—he'd obviously be spending more time there. And while she'd like to think they could live in the same town, she wasn't anxious to see him show up at the local clambake with some girl she'd gone to school with, or worse, some jet-set sophisticate from one of the European jaunts he'd likely go on once he was back on the Murphy Resorts payroll.

She was over him on the condition she didn't have his future rubbed in her face. While she wouldn't call herself a sore loser per se, she was competitive enough to prefer winning.

Darting the rest of the way up the stairs, she stepped onto the deck and headed for the helm. Night air blew over her, the temperatures out on the water decidedly cool even though the day had been gorgeous back home on the Cape. Sea breezes dotted her cheek with cool moisture, the taste of the salt spray on her lips reminding her of Jack's skin. Ignoring the hum of residual pleasure that memory brought, she bent to check the chart plotter and the headings he'd set. Thankfully, Jack didn't try to stop her. She didn't think she could handle any more touching. Her body still sang with the seductive contact from earlier.

"We're going to Bar Harbor," Jack told her finally, since the high-tech gadgetry wasn't giving up any obvious clues. He checked a few instruments and made an adjustment to some stray dial. "Keith and I traded boats tonight after we got into a BS argument about who had the better vessel. Dumb guy stuff."

Alicia whirled around to face him. She wondered how he could stand the wind with no shirt on, but then, he'd practically been born on a boat. He looked like a gorgeous Poseidon with his granite wedge of shoulders and his dark brown hair blowing in the breeze. He'd pulled on a pair of trousers, which were unbuttoned at his waist, a hint of dark cotton boxers showing through the open V above the fly.

And whoa. How did her eyes end up on that southward journey? She yanked her gaze back to his tanned skin and the crinkle of tiny lines around his eyes that spoke of long days outdoors. They'd been there even when he was younger—he had a smile that lit up his whole expression, but it was one that she'd been privy to only for a single incredible year. The lines were deeper now, as if they'd been baked in by the sun from all those months on a destroyer in the Pacific.

"So if you told him you had a better boat than him, how exactly did you end up sailing his out of the marina while I was sleeping?" Keith had told her to make herself comfortable because he'd be late arriving. Had he set her up for this? Her stomach dropped at the thought that he would do something so underhanded when she'd believed they were friends.

"Hmm…" Jack scrubbed a hand over his jaw. "I might have taunted him about not knowing how to sail. I mean, will you look at this thing?" He gestured to the top-notch equipment at the helm. The tiny hot tub built into the foredeck. "How does this floating house party bear any resemblance to boating as we know it?"

For a moment, the "we" sucked her in, included her in that exclusive little club of insiders that Jack respected. His list had always been short, his high standards tough for most mortals to meet. When she had been among the people Jack trusted, the feeling had been awfully damn good for a girl who'd grown up without the mother who'd left long ago, and with a father more committed to his job than his kids. Jack Murphy had once seemed like Prince Charming, there to save the day.

Not anymore.

"So you didn't want to take his party cruiser, but you were so dead set on forcing him to sail a *real man's* boat that you swapped vessels." She was starting to form a picture now. She could almost hear the conversation at Ryan's party. "And what do you think Keith's motive was for taking you up on the trade when he knew damn well I would be on board?"

A gust of wind blew the bedspread open around her legs, the fabric lifting clear up to her hip. She battled it back down, stuffing the excess fabric between her knees to pin it in place.

She thought she spied a flash of male appreciation in Jack's eyes before he recovered the glower that now seemed to be his trademark expression around her.

"I can't imagine what he was thinking, but you can bet I'm going to find out." He waved his phone again.

"If you even get a cell signal out here." She sighed. "Look, why don't we just tuck into land wherever we are and I'll catch a bus to Bar Harbor. No harm, no foul."

She moved back toward the hatch to return downstairs and dress. She didn't need this kind of garbage in her life. Whatever Keith had in mind by throwing her together with Jack tonight, it wasn't going to work. Any chance of making peace between them had ended when he'd signed up for the navy the second he'd finished telling her they were through.

It'd been the ultimate kiss-off. Not only had he dumped her, he'd hot-footed it to the other side of the globe and sold himself to Uncle Sam in the process, just to make damn sure she knew how serious he was about getting away from her.

Or at least, that's how it had seemed. And he'd never disabused her of the notion, keeping his explanations to a bare minimum in a way that had hurt like hell.

"No." Jack's arms were around her, stopping her.

It didn't make sense, because she could see how much of a hardship it was for him to be near her. To touch her. Most guys would have at least let her dream on in her aroused state when they'd been in bed together, but Mr. Noble and Upstanding had been too honorable to cop an extra ten-second feel, bolting out of bed as if she was a pariah.

So why did he have his arms around her now?

"Excuse me?" Her hair whipped about her face in a crosswind and she had to push it aside so she could see him.

"I will take you to Bar Harbor." His hands warmed her right through the quilt fabric. The rest of her remained chilled, while two perfect imprints of his palms flared hot on her forearms. "I have to go there anyhow to drop off the boat for Keith's colleague."

"That doesn't mean we ought to travel together." How could she survive being penned up on a boat with her controlling, I-know-best ex-boyfriend? Not in this lifetime. "In fact, that's the worst idea I've ever heard."

He turned her out of the wind, taking most of it on his back and shielding her from the light spray the gusts kicked up. He was protective like that. Always had been. Some would call that thoughtful. But there came a point where a woman didn't want to be wound up in bubble wrap for safekeeping, and somehow Jack had never understood that about her. He'd told her she shouldn't wait for him while he was in the navy, since it would be too much to expect of her.

Another way he'd cut her to the core.

"You didn't think it was such a bad idea ten minutes ago when we were in bed together."

She'd need a crowbar to pry her jaw off the deck.

"You did not just say that to me," she managed to reply finally, her throat cracking on a dry note at the reminder of how she'd been drawn to him like a magnet. "I was *asleep*. Are you going to hold it against me that I was having some anonymous sexy dream?"

"It was hardly anonymous. You said my name."

"Did I?" She vaguely recalled this. "I wouldn't know what I said or did because I was *sleeping*."

"Would you like me to remind you?" His hands shifted ever so subtly on her arms, the play of his fingers up her shoulders taking the touch from gentle restraint to… Sensual? Romantic?

She didn't know how to define it—the last time she'd checked, Jack Murphy had told her to have a nice life, since they clearly weren't meant for each other. The news had come after their umpteenth argument about how to make a relationship work while she was still in college and he was globe-trotting for his father's company. He'd ditched her and the family job in one swoop, encouraging her to date guys her own age since he was "tying her down," preventing her from having a real college experience.

"You. Wouldn't. Dare." She knew him well enough to know he would never use her attraction against her. He was all about protectiveness. Doing what was best for her even when she'd hated it.

As his eyes narrowed, a dangerous light glittered in their depths. Too late she realized she'd just issued a challenge to a man who'd never known how to walk away from one.

2

HE WOULDN'T DARE?

Jack suspected she didn't have any idea what he would dare when it came to her.

Alicia LeBlanc had transformed from a sweet college coed in need of a date for her fall formal, to a sexual dynamo with an attitude.

He didn't know what to make of this woman who bore little resemblance to the studious business major she'd once been, or even the hardworking swimmer and sorority girl he remembered from before he'd joined the navy. But he didn't feel the same limits with her as he had four years ago, that was for damn certain.

She'd grown even more beautiful, her athletic body still trim and lean but the curves subtly more voluptuous. Long blond waves fell around her shoulders. She wasn't as tall as most swimmers, but she had a can't-miss presence when she walked into a room. A throaty laugh you could hear across a crowded party. The abundance of freckles across her nose reminded him that as an avid diver and surfer, she loved the outdoors as much as he did. She'd started giving lessons in a variety of water sports during her senior year of college and had grown the business to include equipment rentals and a couple of employees.

Hell, she'd been game for any sport he'd ever wanted to play, and that was saying something. Most guys he knew couldn't handle the mega-competitive weekend reunions at the Murphy household, but Alicia hadn't just sat on the sidelines flipping burgers. She'd tried her hand as starting pitcher when they'd played stickball, and got prickly when her receivers hadn't run the routes she'd dictated when they'd let her quarterback a team in the Turkey Bowl. She had a natural competitiveness that made her fit right in with his family.

If she hadn't been so damn young—or maybe if she hadn't been every bit as strong-willed as him—they might have gotten somewhere. But both those things had tripped them up and he hadn't thought it would be fair to maintain the relationship when he'd made the decision to take a navy contract after...well, when the call to serve had become undeniably personal.

He hadn't been at liberty to discuss the way the war had hit close to home back then. Couldn't let her in on why he'd needed to sign that contract so badly. And the secrecy had cost them both.

He'd heard she'd dated half his high-school graduating class since then—okay, two other guys that he knew about. But she'd dated with enough of a vengeance that she'd shown him she didn't care about the breakup.

It'd stung when he'd gotten the news on his first stint overseas, back when he'd been sitting on a ship in the Gulf of Oman.

"I'm going to give you fair warning, Alicia." He kept his hands on her, ill prepared to deal with the riptide effect of being alone with her for the first time in four years. He was too exhausted—and too turned on from finding himself in bed with her. "Because even though I play to win, I believe in a level playing field."

"How generous of you." The soft words held plenty of sarcasm, but she didn't move a muscle, her body perfectly still under his hands.

"I would dare a lot when it comes to you." Because he'd never forgotten about her. Because she'd moved on with an ease that had rankled long afterward. "So if you won't admit you felt something for me in the cabin earlier, I'm not going to think twice about proving what a lie that is."

"Okay, so I felt something, damn it," she snapped, leaning forward to get in his face. "Satisfied?"

Her gutsiness had always made her irresistible. And he had no reason to hold back now. She'd sparked a flame inside him and he couldn't think of any reason not to follow it to its natural conclusion. Maybe this time it would burn itself out, since trying to shut it down four years ago had backfired. He'd thought about her more than any other woman he'd ever been with, probably because he'd stomped out the relationship too soon.

They might not have personalities that meshed for

the long term. But they sure as hell had chemistry that would light things up in the here and now.

Damn it, they needed to find out what was between them once and for all.

"No. Admit it was for me. You were dreaming about me. You said my name."

She pursed her lips. Brown eyes narrowed. Everything about her posture told him she would argue this all night. So he opted for a preemptive strike. Winding one arm around her waist and one around her back, he drew her to him. Her hands still clutched the blanket to her neck, so he pinned them between his chest and hers. Captive.

Her eyes went wide in the reflected glow of the running lights. Surprised. He could feel the rapid tattoo of her heartbeat against his chest. And he had no qualms about fitting his mouth to hers and tasting her lips.

The flavor of her damn near took out his knees. Familiar and foreign all at once, her mouth followed his. Part of him couldn't believe she was here, in his arms, allowing him to touch her and kiss her. But they'd always been good together physically. And even though he'd been dead to the world when he'd fallen into that berth earlier, he could have sworn she'd been aware it was him she was touching.

He hadn't been positive she'd said his name at all, half afraid he'd dreamed up all that heat radiating from her when she'd rubbed her thigh against his. Licked him. But now, feeling her mouth come alive under his, he knew he'd been right. The spark between them was still there.

Without warning, she broke the kiss and stepped back. Ocean air blew between them, cooling his hot skin and stirring the blanket she gripped around her as if it were a life vest.

"Uncle." One hand lifted to her mouth, as if to stroke away his kiss. Or to preserve the feel of it? "Okay? You win. I must have known on some level it was you in bed because I thought I was dreaming about you. But you have to believe that I never would have started coming on to you if I'd been awake. It's been four years and a lot of water under the bridge."

He did *not* want to think about the water under the bridge. The other guys she'd dated. The feelings for her that had run deep even after they broke up. He rerouted his thoughts with an effort.

"Subconsciously, you still want me." Personally, he thought the desire was pretty obvious on the surface, too, or she wouldn't have returned his kiss just now. But he recalled she had pride as fierce as his own, and he didn't think pushing any harder right now would be wise.

"Or maybe I have a selective memory when I'm sleeping, and I can choose to remember your positive attributes instead of that famous Murphy arrogance." She tucked into the stairwell. "I'm going below. It's freezing up here."

Funny. He'd been plenty warm until she'd walked away. After one more quick glance to check the horizon for traffic, Jack followed her down into the galley. She slid into a seat at the built-in table near the bag of supplies he'd picked up on his way to the marina.

He took the seat across from her, giving her space without letting go of a conversational point that needed to be settled ASAP.

"You're right about the arrogance," he admitted, eyes adjusting to the green tinge of the night-light he'd left on in the hall. "But I only pushed the kiss to remind you that we're not exactly strangers. I mean, you trusted Keith enough to take you to Bar Harbor, and that guy couldn't sail his way out of a bathtub. So why not me?"

She laughed. The warm, throaty chuckle pleased his insides like hot chocolate after a snowball war. Damn, but she was gorgeous when she smiled.

"The fact that I can still be persuaded to kiss you after you dumped me right before my spring formal and then joined the navy to escape my wrath sort of makes me wary around you." The humor in her tone was tinged with a dark edge that surprised him.

But then, shipping out weeks after their breakup had guaranteed he wouldn't see the fallout. Of course, she didn't know that his decision to go into the service hadn't been about her.

"The timing was unfortunate," he admitted, unprepared to discuss those darker days with her. "But don't let an old argument prevent you from making this trip. With two of us to sail this monstrosity that Keith calls a boat, we'll make decent time, and you'll be off and running in Bar Harbor before you know it."

Her gaze turned thoughtful. Serious.

And the fact that he seemed to be holding his breath clued him in to how much he wanted her to say yes. A smarter man might have questioned his sanity, given the way they'd hurt each other in the past. But seeing her again had blasted through old defenses, sparking a need to simply be with her.

"Maybe a little closure would be a good thing." She toyed with the plastic handle of the shopping bag on the table. "I've missed your family parties."

"Still flying high on the year you won the Turkey Bowl?"

"I threw a bomb to Kyle and he ran it into the end zone for the big finish." She mimicked the throw, her arm reaching out of the blanket long enough to give him a glimpse of soft, feminine curves beneath. "It was one of my finer moments."

They stared at each other across the polished wooden table. Was she remembering the finer moment that came afterward, when they'd stolen into one of the cabanas so he could help her celebrate her victory? He'd insisted that she deserved a reward she wouldn't forget....

"I—" He cleared his throat, knowing she didn't want to hear about that right now. First, he had to get her to agree to this trip with him. "Yeah. I remember."

Needing a distraction from memories that lambasted him, he grabbed the bag of supplies on the table and dragged it closer.

"You hungry?" he asked.

He sure as hell was. But there wasn't anything in that bag that could help.

"Starving, actually." She tucked her legs up on the bench beneath her. "Some of us didn't get invited to the engagement party of the century at the Murphy Mansion. How was it?"

Grateful to reroute his thoughts, he realized she probably would like to hear about Ryan's shindig. There'd been six months where she'd practically been family, after all.

She'd moved to Chatham when he was in high school, but he hadn't really become aware of her until he'd seen her at one of Kyle's football games, cheering on the sidelines and explaining the finer points of the game—a little impatiently—to some girlfriends. He'd been amused by her solid grip on the offense's use of the "I" formation, but she'd been five years his junior, way too young to register on his dating radar.

But once he'd become aware of her, Alicia LeBlanc seemed to be everywhere he turned for the next two years. Leading her high school team to a state championship in swimming and earning a college scholarship. Taking an interest in the hospitality field and getting a summer internship in one of his father's resorts as an activity assistant. Showing up at his parents' house in the summers with a slew of Kyle and Axel's other friends to boat and surf.

Jack had become annoyed with himself when he realized he was heading home on the weekends just to see her, and he'd made a hell of an effort to stay away, knowing she was still too young for him. Not in terms of years, but in terms of where they were in life. She was still getting her education, while he was out on his own, taking trips to Europe for his job as VP of global properties.

He'd succeeded in putting distance between them right up until her junior year, when she'd pitched in to handle the PR for a charity golf tournament at one of his father's resorts when the promotions director had been sick. Jack had been drafted by the family to help her, since he'd been in town. And seeing her in that light—professional and capable—had forced him to stop thinking of her as a kid. Still, he wouldn't have acted on the attraction if she hadn't come to him out on the golf course when he'd been picking up the flag sticks that night with his brother Ryan.

Ryan had read the signals and left them alone, but not before daring Jack to make a move on her.

Alicia had him outmaneuvered even then, making a no-holds-barred play for him on the ninth hole. And she'd been as assertive on a personal level as she'd always been on the playing field....

"The party was—" He shrugged. "I don't know. Food was good." He pulled a six-pack of drinks from the bag and a few snacks. "But it can't compare to grape soda and chocolate Pop-Tarts."

"Perfect." She snagged the box from him and opened it while he retrieved a glass and poured her drink over ice.

Then he filled a second one for himself.

"So…cheers to our northern voyage?" He kept her glass hostage while she thought about it.

"You're impossible." She chewed her pastry and narrowed her gaze again. "You know I can't eat this without something to wash it down."

"Guess you'd better hurry up and see we're going to make this trip together."

Still she left him hanging.

"We ought to sketch out some ground rules," she said finally, setting her snack back on the foil package.

"You think that's necessary?" He didn't like the sound of "rules" when it came to her. He'd imposed a list as long as his arm where she was concerned in the past, and look how that had turned out.

"First—" she held up a finger, ignoring his question "—no kissing."

He resisted the urge to roll his eyes. She was going with him, right? He'd have to find more imaginative ways to make her remember how good they could be together.

He nodded.

"Second." Her middle finger joined the pointer. "Separate beds."

"What kind of guy do you think I am?"

"It doesn't hurt to spell out our expectations."

"You're just scared you'll jump me again if we end up between the sheets." Begrudgingly, he handed her the soda, hoping the list was almost done. "I'm afraid to hear the rest of the rules."

"There's just one more." She set the drink on the

table between them. "I really debated on this last item. Should rule number three be that you wear a shirt all the time?"

He couldn't have held back his grin if his life depended on it. He'd definitely spend this trip half-dressed.

"What's the alternative?"

"That you occasionally let me steer the ship." Folding her arms, she planted her elbows on the table. For all intents and purposes it looked as if she was staring him down.

"I already told you I'm glad to have another hand on deck." He knew she couldn't read all the controls on the helm, but she'd been on enough boats to spot him if he wanted a rest.

"You have a hard time giving up control," she reminded him. Absently, she spun the grape soda on the table, almost as if to remind him she could walk away from this deal at any moment. "I'd like some assurance that I can weigh in on the captain's decisions."

"You want to second-guess me."

"They're good rules, Jack." She picked up her glass and tipped it in his direction. "What do you say?"

"I say cheers." He clinked his drink to hers before she could change her mind. "Bon voyage."

Taking a sip, she eyed him warily over the rim.

"I certainly hope so."

SEATED ON THE FORWARD deck the next morning, the fall sun warming her face as they sped through wide-open blue sea, Alicia wondered if she would have made the same decision to sail with Jack by the clear light of day. With hours between waking up in bed with him and making her choice.

She couldn't pretend the attraction between them hadn't played into her agreeing to go with him to Bar Harbor. No matter how much she told herself she'd gotten over him, feeling her heart race at his presence, experiencing the sharp hunger for him that she'd never had for another man, had urged her to find out what the heck had gone so wrong between them. How did they end up so hurt and angry with each other? And why had the universe dropped this irresistible man in her path— for a second time—when they were too stubborn to get along?

Maybe relationships were like swimming. Practice enough, and eventually you improved your times. Not that she planned to practice with Jack Murphy. He'd crushed her heart enough for one lifetime, thank you very much. But perhaps she could discover what had really sent him running four years ago. Because all that BS about her being too young? Total smoke screen. She hadn't bought it then and she didn't buy it now.

She peered over one shoulder to where he manned the wheel, looking like a modern-day pirate with a blue-and-white bandanna tied around his head and a day's growth of beard on his jaw. He wore khaki cargoes and a white linen shirt that he'd neglected to button much higher than his navel. The fabric flapped in the breeze as they cut through the waves.

He'd slept off and on after sunrise, giving the wheel to her and showing her the most basic navigation skills so he could catch up on some rest. After they'd made their pact the night before, she'd fallen into a hard sleep until dawn, while Jack had taken the night shift at the helm. Now, well past noon, he was back in charge of the boat and she was faced with the consequences of her late-night agreement with him.

Noticing her looking his way, he grinned.

"Regretting the no-kissing rule already, aren't you?" he called over the noise of the engine.

"Hardly." She was actually patting herself on the back for that one. No sense giving him any advantages when the man had too much to work with already. "I was just wondering when I should let you in on my real reason for agreeing to this trip with you."

She wouldn't, of course. Jack was probably at the top of the list of men in his family who wouldn't appreciate soul-searching in the name of self-improvement—or in the name of enlightening an old girlfriend. Although possibly he'd share that top slot with his brother Daniel—the family rebel. At least the other brothers had learned how to put a socially acceptable facade atop all the he-man aggressiveness that ran in the family.

"What do you mean?" Jack's frown was so pronounced it would probably leave wrinkles.

Well, now she'd have to tell him something....

Pushing to her feet, she scooted along the wooden walkway that circled the bow, and stepped down into the saloon area behind the helm. There was a built-in settee and table under a hardtop cover that provided protection from the sun in hot weather or kept the captain out of the wind on a cooler voyage.

"I figured it would be a good idea to pick your brain about opening a bed-and-breakfast in a new town. I would have quizzed Keith about it if he'd taken me on this trip, but since I've got you…"

"You can pick all you want, but I'm no expert anymore." He settled in the captain's chair, sitting sideways to talk to her. The boat easily handled the small swells of the warm September afternoon in the Atlantic, and didn't need too much attention. "I quit my job at Murphy Resorts when I went into the service."

"But rumor has it you've started investing in bars all over the Cape. Sounds to me like you've still got a hand in the hospitality industry."

"I figured I'd keep my money in the local economy while I chart my next move. It's been an adjustment since coming out of the service."

Surprised at the admission from a man who rarely admitted anything in life had ever been difficult for him, Alicia left the comment alone for now. Had he liked navy life? Maybe he'd been drawn to it for more reasons than just an escape.

And damn, but didn't it paint her as self-centered for never having considered that before? Curiosity niggled.

"Active in your dad's business or not, you know a lot about the hospitality scene." She tapped a fingernail on the plastic tabletop, inhaling the clean scent of the ocean. "What things would you look for in a bed-and-breakfast at a new location?"

She'd take advice wherever she could get it, since she was determined to make a go of this business on her own, away from her father's continued insistence that he knew what was best for her.

"B and Bs are a whole different ball game than the resorts my family have specialized in," Jack cautioned, signaling to a sleek superyacht that cruised past, dwarfing them.

"I'm very aware of that. Go out on a limb for me, okay?" As their boat bobbed in the wake of the bigger craft, she was vaguely surprised at his need to downplay his expertise, so at odds with the arrogance she had come to associate with him. What other changes might she uncover during the course of their journey together?

"I'd make sure this market supported other bed-and-breakfast establishments and that they're more than half-full eight months of the year. Then I'd want to know what would make my inn stand out among the competing properties." When he had their boat steadied again, he returned his full attention to her. "B and Bs aren't cash cows. They're labors of love for most people. Are you going to have the income to stay well ahead of the mortgage?"

"I've got a subsidiary income opportunity in mind." She wasn't ready to give up her water-sports business completely. Besides, she needed something to make her property distinctive. She needed this project to succeed.

"What else? Any time of year that's better for openings? And it's an older place with some smaller rooms. Would you combine some of them to make more spacious quarters when finances allow, or pitch the place as 'cozy' and try to make it work with the smaller rooms?"

"Whoa." He left the captain's chair and slid into the seat across from her at the built-in table. The steering controls were still within reach if he stretched. "You're really serious about this? About opening a business on your own in Maine, of all places?"

"Of course I'm serious." She tugged down the brim of the camouflage canvas fishing hat she'd worn to protect her from the sun. She didn't think she had much space left for more freckles. "I've researched this property every way possible without actually seeing it. And what have you got against Maine?"

"It's far away and I've never heard you say anything about wanting to live in Maine."

And since when had they discussed her future? Even when they'd been dating, that had been a topic Jack avoided like the plague.

"Sometimes it's good to put space between yourself and where you grew up, right?" She didn't think he could argue that, considering the choice he'd made.

"Sure. But you love it on the Cape."

As opposed to Jack, who'd spent half the time they were dating on another continent.

"In case you haven't noticed, there's a lot of competition for tourist dollars there. And your family runs a tight ship. I don't think I'm ready to battle with the

Murphy clan in the business world." She'd considered that kind of venture. But it would mean living in Jack's backyard. Circulating in his family's world. "Bad enough I could kick your butt at sports. I couldn't demean you in business as well."

"Ally, I'm serious." He wasn't letting her off the hook about this. "It's going to be tough enough starting a business alone. Why travel so far from your roots to make it happen? Why not give yourself the support system of your friends and family?"

She felt herself stiffen, her pride bristling at the thought of her father or brother coming near her project. But she *had* asked Jack for his input. Damn it, she'd wanted advice about how to handle the inn in Bar Harbor, not all the reasons she shouldn't buy it. She tipped her face into the ocean breeze and took a deep breath to try to soften her tone.

"My family is a far cry from yours, Jack." Her father was a workaholic who'd driven her mom away long ago with his tunnel-vision dedication to his job and his habit of manipulating his kids like chess pieces. Her older brother, and only sibling, had stuck around. But he seemed content to follow in their father's footsteps, commuting daily into Boston or New York to a job that required most of his time.

When her brother wasn't working overtime to add to his bottom line, he indulged in his favorite hobby— telling Alicia how to live her life.

"But they interfere because they love you. You know

that. I think you'll miss being able to see them." Jack's green eyes appeared sincere, his expression heartfelt.

A less wise woman might believe his worry on her behalf *was* sincere. But she understood that it wasn't concern for her needs so much as an unrelenting belief that he knew what was best for everyone around him. Just as her father and her brother did.

"While I appreciate you looking out for me, I'm not asking for help with the personal aspect of this." As long as she liked the property as much in person as she did online, and could get the bank on board, she was closing this deal.

"Have you even thought seriously about opening a place on the Cape, where you have connections?"

Behind him, the ship radio squawked with a weather warning that made Jack check the sky and his watch. The storm clouds might be a few hours away, but as far as Alicia was concerned, Jack was already trying to rain on her parade.

"What connections?" She shook her head. "I couldn't afford a place on the Cape even if I wanted to stay there."

"I'll back you," he announced, rising from the built-in table to make adjustments on the boat's automatic steering system.

She wished her life had an auto steering function right about now because she was feeling more adrift by the moment, and Jack seemed determined to step in and take charge.

"You'll back me?" She parroted back the offer to

be sure she'd heard correctly. "As in vouch for me to some corporate banker so I can borrow the bazillion dollars it would cost for a nice B and B property on the Cape? Even if you could convince someone to say yes, I wouldn't be able to make a profit fast enough to pay that off. I don't want that kind of pressure."

Most of all, she didn't want to be in debt to Jack.

"No pressure." He turned the boat hard toward the west as he settled into the captain's chair. "The loan would be from me."

For a second, she couldn't catch her breath. Her throat felt as if she'd inhaled a bug off the breeze.

"You can't be serious." How could he even consider such a thing? As tempting as it was to have the budget for a property that could be three times as profitable as the place she was looking at in Maine, she could never do business with her ex.

Out of the question.

He was jumping into her life and trying to take over. And they'd been back in each other's presence for how long? Less than twenty-four hours.

"I've already invested in a handful of places around the Cape and you're a safer risk than some of them." He gestured toward a control on the helm. "Can you flip that switch up?"

Rising to her feet, she joined him by the helm and noticed from the chart plotter that he was headed toward Marina Bay, just south of Boston.

"Where are we going?" Frowning, she remembered how tough it was to keep up with a man who didn't share his plans or intentions, a man who plowed through life on his own terms.

"Storm's coming. It'll be safer to go inland for the night."

"Fine. You get to steer the boat, after all." She ground her teeth together, trying to remain gracious. Patient. "But you're not steering my life, and I'm still going to Bar Harbor to buy an inn. Alone."

She turned to make sure he got the message, and found they were closer than she thought. He'd stood beside the captain's chair to snap a clear side curtain into place around the helm.

"Sure," he agreed easily before thrusting half the vinyl fabric into her arms. "We can talk about it over dinner."

Helping him spread out the material so they could fasten it on the side behind her, she reached high over her head to connect the snaps even though the sun was still shining.

"Dinner?" Her stomach growled on cue as he finished the snaps on his side and leaned in to assist her with hers.

Her hip grazed his thigh as their arms tangled at the task. Warmth sparked over her skin, her body clearly impressed with his. Then again, she'd given herself a healthy sample of what he felt like last night in bed. Getting things started without finishing them was bound to leave a woman frustrated.

"Aren't you hungry?" he asked, his fingers slow to

finish the task while they stood so close, their arms raised.

His green eyes turned smoky as he stared down at her, his chest a hairbreadth from her breasts.

Hungry? Try ravenous.

"I could go for something to eat," she admitted, wondering why the sea had to be so calm right now when even a little wave would rock their bodies together. Quench her thirst for a quick feel of him.

"Great. I'll finish this up if you want to get ready. There's a nice Italian place I know right on the water."

It took her a moment to realize he was being the perfect gentleman. Letting her go free without so much as a copped feel. Hastily, she lowered her arms. Tearing her eyes off Jack's chest took a bit longer, but she managed it at last.

Words escaped her, however, and her mouth was too dry to talk, so she settled for a nod before she hurried to the stairs and went below deck.

She *really* needed to get herself together before she went another round with him. She might be older and wiser than she'd been four years ago, but obviously he was, too.

The man's physical chemistry had only grown more potent. She wouldn't have thought such a thing was possible. If she wasn't careful, she'd be back in his bed in no time.

3

FINISHED WITH HIS MEAL, Jack topped off Alicia's wine and then settled into his high-backed club chair, unable to take his eyes off her as she enjoyed the food.

Vicenza's dockside restaurant was quiet tonight, with a handful of seafaring refugees taking shelter from a hard rain. Other than that, patrons were scarce. Which was just fine with him. Their conversation had been private in a corner looking out over Marina Bay, the boats bobbing in the water just beyond the glass. Keith's big gas guzzler was on a slip farther away, banished to a mooring by itself.

But at least they'd made it to port before the worst of the rain came. They were warm and dry inside, while a Spanish guitarist serenaded the handful of guests with Paganini. The guy was seriously good. Yet it wasn't just the music, or the food, or the fire crackling in the oversize hearth in the middle of the room that made Jack happy. Nope. His contentment came from sitting with Alicia, who wore a simple navy blue dress, as she savored the last of her spaghetti alle vongole—that really did it for him.

"I can't stop eating," she explained when she caught him staring at her. "It's so good."

"I'm glad you like it." He pushed his empty plate aside and wished he didn't have to bring up the subject of her bed-and-breakfast yet, since it seemed like a touchy subject for her. He'd rather simply take pleasure in her company. Her enjoyment of the meal.

But they'd be in Bar Harbor in another couple days if they made good time. He couldn't afford to postpone the conversation if it meant she'd move three hundred miles away.

"Whatever you're thinking right now," she said, putting down her fork, "stop."

"Excuse me?" He sat forward in his chair, remembering he needed to stay on his toes with her.

"You heard me." She all but pointed an accusing finger at him. "You get this crinkle right here…." She reached across the table to sketch a finger down the center of his forehead. "I know whenever you have that furrow it bodes no good for me."

"And you're basing that on…what? Dating experiences from four years ago?"

"That, along with new evidence I've gathered. For instance, when you discovered I was sleeping in your bed—" she pointed to her forehead "—crinkle. Then, when you decided I hadn't looked into the logistics of running a bed-and-breakfast far from home—bam." Again she flashed her finger to her forehead.

"Funny you mention that, because I think you'd find a lot of success on the Cape—"

"Jack?" She cut him off. "Unless there's some hidden plumbing problem or obvious damage to the place that I couldn't see in the photos, I'm buying that inn and moving to Bar Harbor. End of story."

He shook his head. "But you asked for my input on the move. How come you won't listen to any advice now?"

"I wanted advice on how to run a successful inn in Bar Harbor, not a barrage of reasons why you think I'm going to fail." She peered out over the stormy water, thoughtful for a moment. "I'm not a college kid anymore, Jack. You can't dictate how my future unfolds now that you're not a part of it. Besides, I've fought too hard against my father's and my brother's efforts to manage my life to simply roll over when someone tells me to. I make my own decisions."

There was nothing feisty about it. No challenge. No threat. She remained utterly matter-of-fact. Which made him realize how seriously she took this choice. She planned to make tracks away from the Cape and start over somewhere else—somewhere far from…him.

The news rocked Jack. Up until now, he'd thought she was just having an adventure—dreaming big, maybe gathering ideas for a far-off someday. But she wasn't at the dreamer stage of her life anymore. She'd matured. Changed. Become a woman with plans and goals that didn't have squat to do with him.

If he was going to have any shot at another chance with her, he'd need to act fast.

"You're right." He nodded slowly. "I'm sure you've given this a lot of thought. But I can't help notice the timing of the move—me returning home and you lighting out of town before I even had the chance to look you up. Should I take that personally?"

She shifted in her seat, leaning back to regard him curiously. "You wouldn't have had any reason to look me up and you know it. We were through in no uncertain terms four years ago, and as much as it hurt, I did recover."

Seeing her again, wanting her again, made him wonder if *he* had recovered. It had been easier to tell himself the breakup was the right move when he'd had the distance of half a world between them.

"I would have hunted you down sooner or later." He'd be kidding himself to think anything else. His brother had only hastened the inevitable by setting them up for this trip together.

Their eyes met. Held. This time, it wasn't just about physical attraction. A wealth of memories—good and bad—flowed in like high tide.

"Can I get you folks anything else?" a perky waitress in black slacks and a white tuxedo shirt prompted, hands ready to clear their plates.

The interruption broke the moment. Alicia shook her head, straightening in her chair as the waitress tidied the table. After a brief debate over splitting the bill that made him grind his teeth, Jack paid and escorted his traveling companion to the door.

They stood in the foyer as rain pounded on the low tin roof of the porch add-on that served as extra summer seating. He could still hear strains of the Spanish guitar and a few laughs from the kitchen where the extra wait-staff milled around on a night with few customers.

"Did you want to try sleeping on the boat in this weather, or would you rather look for a hotel nearby?" He'd spent enough time on the water that a few waves wouldn't bother him, but he wasn't sure what her tolerance was.

The only time they'd weathered a storm together while boating, they had pulled into a sandy cove and passed the time making love in the rain.

"I'll be fine on the boat." Alicia tucked her purse under her arm to prepare for the sprint to the dock where they'd tied the craft.

"I can move the boat away from the slip once we get on board so we're not bumping the pier all night. It shouldn't be bad if we anchor farther out." Sliding off his jacket, he gave it to her. "You can use this to keep dry."

She shook her head. "I'll just run fast."

Reaching for the door, she headed out into the storm. Even before they left the shelter of the overhang, the rain was hitting the ground with such force it splashed water on their feet. Not wanting to argue with her, Jack tucked her under his arm and held the jacket over them both like a tent.

"Be careful!" He pointed to the wet surface below their feet. "The planks turn slick in the rain."

When she didn't seem inclined to argue, he relaxed enough to let himself enjoy the feel of her at his side. She fit perfectly, her head tipped against his chest. The curve of her hip was a natural spot to put his hand.

The downpour pattered loud white noise, confining their world to the square foot of space under the stretch of silk-lined Italian wool. When they reached the spot where the pier connected to the concrete walkway, a huge puddle loomed, so he lifted her a few inches off the ground and carried her over it.

"Put me down!" she protested automatically, although he noticed her lip curled at the prospect of landing in the miniature pond he waded through to reach the dock.

"Don't knock the chivalry, Ally. I could have gone caveman with the carry." He would rather draw her closer and press her body full-frontal to his instead of hitching her up against his hip.

Still, the contact lifted her enough that her breast molded to the side of his chest, the soft warmth a welcome bonus for his trouble.

When he set her on her feet on the other side of the puddle, she sprinted out from under his jacket like a runner off the blocks.

Damn it.

He broke into a run to follow, stuffing his coat under one arm. Annoyed, he started to call out a warning about the planks when she slowed down to grab a

stainless steel rail on the stern above the swim platform of the catamaran. Gracefully, she stepped aboard,
seemingly oblivious to the driving deluge. Already her
blond hair was drenched to a dripping light brown. Her
soaked blue dress cleaved to her body like a second
skin.

Reminding him all over again of that storm they'd
waited out on a beach off the Cape. She'd looked just
like that in her wet T-shirt and jean shorts, her string
bikini showing through the top until he'd ditched that
and everything else to be inside her....

"What are you thinking?" She was studying his face,
he realized, watching him intently as he came aboard.

Perhaps some of his thoughts showed in his expression.

"You mean you can't tell from reading the crinkles?"
He made an offhanded gesture to his forehead, then
started untying the boat from the dock.

"No." She shoved her purse under the covering at
the helm and stepped out onto the foredeck to pull in
the bolsters that protected the boat from rubbing up
against the slip. "I can't remember seeing that expression before. But it's been four years. You were bound
to add to your repertoire."

She wanted to know what he'd been thinking? Well,
he was inclined to share. Especially since she was
moving three hundred miles away from him. Why not
put it all on the line during this trip, so she could at least
see how badly he still wanted her?

It might not make any difference to her decision.

And it probably shouldn't, since they'd been like oil and water even at the best of times. But they'd ended on such a crappy note four years ago. Maybe this time together could heal the mistakes he'd made with her back then, and allow them both to move on without bitterness and unresolved feelings.

Of course, that could be one giant rationalization to touch her again.

"I was thinking about the last time you and I were out on the water together in a storm." He tucked away the rope that he'd pulled in from the mooring.

Standing, he moved closer as one of the bumpers slipped from her grip and fell back into the bay with a splash.

He bent to retrieve it, her tanned legs within tempting reach. She didn't move, eyeing him as he stood, the two of them closer than they'd been since the night before.

When he'd kissed her.

"It was a lot hotter that day," Alicia reminded him, tearing her gaze away from his to peer up at the sky. "I don't think it would be wise to get naked in this kind of weather."

Just hearing her say the word *naked* was a turn-on. Then again, everything about her juiced him up.

"Although we do have a built-in hot tub to take the chill off." He pointed toward the absurd little whirlpool tucked into the foredeck of Keith's cushy watercraft.

As much as he'd like to pull her against him and remind her how fun it would be to tangle limbs for a while, Jack sidestepped around her to finish untying the boat. No pressure. Judging from the way she'd moved against him in bed last night, she remembered well enough what it could be like between them. It was just a matter of getting her to see that they could indulge that attraction without all the heartache of the last time.

Pleasure only. Pure and simple.

ALICIA COULD TELL she wasn't dealing with the same old Jack Murphy anymore.

The man she knew would have reminded her in vivid detail of that last time they'd been together in the rain. He wouldn't have stopped the trip down memory lane until she was panting and begging for more. She had every faith he could accomplish this even without kissing her—his fingers were incredibly talented.

In fact, she'd had visions of him walking his fingertips up her bare leg moments ago when he'd fished the bumper out of the water. But he'd moved along like the consummate gentleman, leading her to wonder what had become of the man she once knew. Shades of the old take-charge and I-know-what's-best Jack were still visible in the way he'd tried to discourage her from the Bar Harbor project—right down to investing in a bed-and-breakfast on the Cape for her.

But he hadn't tried to touch her all day—even though he'd obviously been thinking about it—which revealed an intriguing level of restraint he hadn't possessed in the past. Heck, she wasn't sure if *she* had enough re-

straint to keep her hands to herself for two more days
at sea.

Now, heedless of the rain, she remained above deck
with him as he freed the boat and pushed away from
the dock. Firing up the engine, he maneuvered carefully
to avoid the next pier over, but the slip he'd taken was
isolated enough to make quick work of it.

She watched the depth finder as he motored slowly
away from the harbor. At twenty-six feet, he let the
anchor out, pulling against it with the engine to ensure
it set properly.

"Did the navy teach you anything about boats you
didn't already know?" she asked once he cut the motor.

Tucked under the hardtop covering the helm, they
were protected from the worst of the rain but not the
cool air. She shivered in her wet dress.

"Only the kinds with weapons." He flipped off a few
other switches, dimming the ambient light from the in-
strument panel. He left a white light on so other boats
could see them, but the mist over the water dimmed the
brightness to a dull glow.

When nothing more seemed to be forthcoming about
his time in the service—a time that remained a mystery
to her—she couldn't help a twinge of disappointment.

"Hopefully, we won't need to take any evasive ma-
neuvers in Marina Bay."

"I'll keep you safe, Ally." Jack's green eyes were serious, his stare inciting a warmth that made her shiver.

He must have noticed, because he gestured toward

the stairs leading below deck. "You can shower first. You must be cold."

"A little." She rubbed the soaked arms of her simple dress. "But you mentioned a hot tub?" She peered meaningfully toward the covered circle in the foredeck. "I know you must think that's ridiculously frivolous on a boat, but when in Rome…"

"…do as my heathen brother does," he finished, a disparaging note in his voice. But she gathered it was directed toward Keith and not her.

"I'll make sure the water's hot for you," he said.

Grateful he hadn't made her feel completely hedonistic, she headed for the stairs, eager to immerse herself in bubbles. Normally, she wasn't a bubbles kind of woman, but this hadn't been a normal sort of day.

"I'll grab a towel." She could always put it under the hardtop so it stayed dry.

Padding down the stairs out of the rain, she pulled off her shoes and set them aside. Good thing she'd brought a bathing suit, even though she'd never guessed the boat would have such an amenity. After rifling through her suitcase, she pulled on the tankini top and the boy-shorts bottoms, one of her more frivolous suits. For water sports, she favored straightforward racing tanks. But the tankini was a little more showy. It was dark out, but for good measure, she wrapped the towel around her like a robe.

No sense having Jack misconstrue her motives for the hot-tub dip.

Hurrying back up the stairs, she spied him out on the

foredeck, leaning over the uncovered tub. He'd turned a light on inside it so the whirlpool looked like a frothy white cauldron bubbling away in the middle of the boat, bathing him in a soft glow as he checked the gauges.

Rain plastered his dress shirt to his back, the fabric all but transparent, delineating every muscle and striation of his back and shoulders. He'd rolled up his sleeves, revealing forearms sprinkled with dark hair. His profile had a fallen-angel appeal in the white light, his strong features softened by that dimple at the center of his squared chin. He had another dimple when he grinned, but it was fickle, making rare appearances in one cheek when something genuinely amused him.

Seeing him there, looking as if he'd just emerged from the sea, reminded her of what he'd said earlier— about the last time they'd been out on a boat during a storm. That day had been electric, burned into her memory in perfect detail like an elaborate tattoo. Their hunger for each other had been bottomless, the need strong and driving, just like his thrusts as he'd locked her legs around his waist….

Yikes.

She blinked away the image to focus on the present. And promptly encountered a new dilemma as she hid under the hardtop at the helm. If she left her towel here to stay dry, she'd have to dash out onto the foredeck in her bathing suit. And with Jack leaning over the edge of the small pool, she'd feel uncomfortable prancing around half-dressed.

Practicality won over modesty; she tossed the towel

on the captain's chair and darted out onto the deck. Alicia had a brief glimpse of Jack's eyes on her as she dropped down into the pool with a quick splash. That green gaze simmered hotter than the water burbling all around her.

"Ahh." She settled into one of the built-in seats, resting her head against the bolster. "That feels amazing."

The cool rain no longer bothered her as it spattered harmlessly into the hundred-degree water. The tub was deep but narrow. Thankfully, the churning bubbles from the jets hid her body from sight.

"Looks amazing, too." Jack stared at her as he reached into a box behind him and pulled out a longneck. "You want one?"

"What else have you got?" A few minutes ago she wouldn't have thought a cold drink would sound appealing, but she'd be toasty in no time now.

With the stars spilling out overhead and the rich dark of the bay spattered with the occasional navigation lights of a passing craft farther out on the horizon, the night loomed glittering and beautiful.

"Let me see." He turned around, settling the longneck back into a small fridge near the forward seating. "Keith has everything from pomegranate juice to diet Snapple." He pulled up another longneck with an unfamiliar label. "Even a sarsaparilla soda."

"I'll try it." She beckoned for it, her hand meeting his on the cold bottle as he opened the top for her.

The contact spurred a swirl of awareness in her limbs. Deeper.

Pulling the drink closer, she eased away from his touch.

"Do you need anything else?" He made no move to rise, his long legs splayed out on the deck beside the whirlpool as he peered up at the night sky.

She wondered if he could read the stars on a clear night like the old-time sailors. Idly, he ran one hand through the water, his tan skin pale in the ghostly light from the tub. Another shiver pulsed over her skin and this one didn't have a thing to do with being cold.

What would it feel like to have that hand on her body again?

"I should be all set," she assured him, mesmerized by the back-and-forth stroke of his fingers in the water.

He didn't crowd her. Didn't ask to join her. But neither did he leave. They sat together in the rain on the deck, her aching body so close to a hand that knew better than any other how to bring her pleasure. She closed her eyes to try and shut out the visual of his broad palm resting nearby, but that only served to heighten her imagination. Visions of his slick touch skating up her thigh made her breath catch in her throat. Her heart skip a beat.

The quiet settled around her, the rain dulling any sound besides the soft hum of the whirlpool motor. The freshwater scent of the storm softened the usual salty smell of the breeze. Tipping her head back farther on the built-in pillow, she tried to focus on the sky instead of her enigmatic former lover with wickedly talented hands.

"Are you warming up?" he asked finally, his voice closer than it had been before.

She resisted the urge to turn and look at him. They'd agreed there would be no kissing, so the last thing she wanted was to find him too close, too tempting, and end up breaking her own rule. When willpower was scarce, why entice yourself?

"Yes." She stretched her toes out to one of the foot jets, the pulsating action soothing her muscles. "This is great, Jack. Thank you."

Shifting her foot, she let the stream shoot over her ankle, up her calf, until she had to admit the propulsion was more than soothing. In conjunction with Jack's voice in her ear, the tickling pressure was arousing.

The sound returned now, warm and baritone next to her cheek.

"I hear those jets feel even better when you're naked."

The suggestion whispered over her like a teasing caress, her own decadent thoughts spoken aloud. She kept her eyes closed, unable to face him and risk breaking the tenuous connection. She didn't want to return to reality now that she had him beside her again, if only for a few days.

"I'm sure they do," she breathed, so softly she wasn't sure he would even hear.

Should she take this further? There'd been a time when she would have acted on the impulse to strip down for him at that kind of provocation, but she was trying to behave. Be reasonable.

Not get tangled up with him all over again.

Sinking deeper into the water, she aligned another jet between her shoulder blades. The massaging throb against her skin would have been stimulating all on its own, but with the knowledge that Jack was stretched out on the deck behind her, watching her... That propelled the feeling into straight-up erotic territory.

Her back arched with the spray, her breasts breaking the surface and the tops of her shoulders meeting the rim of the tub where his one hand rested. With her eyes closed, the touch was accidental, but she could hardly regret the contact when two of his fingers trailed over her slick skin. He traced the curve of her neck. Skimmed lower to her collarbone, where his touch slipped under the spaghetti strap of her top.

Nudging the fabric to the edge of her shoulder, he pushed it over. Off. Her top remained in place, but it still felt like a major unveiling. Her breath hitched in her throat as pleasure slid through her veins in a thick, heated rush.

"I know you're not ready for more yet, so I'm going to give you some privacy while I take a shower."

He was leaving?

She blinked, unsure if that's what she wanted or not. Of course, she was the one who'd insisted on those damn rules.

Nodding, she swallowed hard and told herself it was just as well that he leave now. Because heaven knew, if he stayed much longer she didn't have a chance of keeping away from him.

"I just have one request before I go." He still spoke softly, but there was a rough quality to his voice now.

She recognized it for what it was—the hunger of holding back. Knowing that it wasn't easy for him to turn away soothed her just a little.

"Mmm?" Imagining what he might ask of her right now, she couldn't envision many requests she wouldn't fill.

But then, that's how she'd ended up naked in the rain with him last time, her legs around his waist as he took her against a tree and made the encounter one of the most sensual moments of her life. She'd never had any restraint when it came to Jack.

Behind her, she heard him get to his feet, and she couldn't resist turning to look at him. But he didn't appear to be stripping down to join her. He stood over her, his powerful body obviously ready for her even in the rain and shadows.

"I hope you think of me when you undress."

Pivoting to walk away, Jack headed for the stairs to his cabin below deck, leaving her more turned on than she'd ever been, and with nothing but a hot tub jet to take the edge off. Frustrated, she stifled a sigh of longing as she watched him go. He wanted to tease her into having more sexy fantasies about him?

Two could play at that game.

4

JACK FIGURED IF HE DIED now, he'd be eligible for sainthood for sure. Walking away from Alicia while she lounged in bubbling water, breathless and ready for his touch, was a feat that ranked close to pushing water uphill. It just went against nature. But he knew she wasn't ready to renew their relationship yet. He'd seen the hesitation in her eyes, even if the rest of her was more than willing.

Now, as he stood under a hot shower in the small cabin bathroom, he thunked his skull against the tile wall. Maybe a cracked skull would help dissipate the visions of Alicia's head thrown back, her body arched toward his touch. He didn't want to make the next move. It didn't seem right to push her when he'd been the one to walk away four years ago. She had to come to him.

Maybe if he'd just stayed on deck a little longer, she would have reached up and dragged him into the tub with her. She could have had her way with him like a ravenous, old-school sea nymph, the kind that sang men to their deaths—hopefully right after sexing him up to a blissed-out place where he forgot his own name.

But no.

He'd had to go all Joe Noble, leaving her to make a well thought-out decision on whether or not to move forward with this brief relationship reprise. The chances of her deciding in his favor would have been about twenty times greater if he'd stayed within touching distance, damn it. Sometimes he was too freaking upstanding to believe.

Speaking of upstanding, the hard-on straining between his thighs had a snowball's chance in hell of finding any real relief tonight without her. He didn't want any part of easing an erection that had her name stamped all over it.

Saint or colossal dumb-ass? He'd have to rethink what category he fell into.

"Jack?" A feminine voice floated through his consciousness, making him pause in the middle of the next round of head pounding.

Remaining still, he listened, pretty sure he'd just imagined her voice the same way he'd been dreaming about her hands all over him. He heard the whoosh of his own breath and the force of the shower stream hitting the tile.

"Jack?" Her voice returned, accompanied by a knock on the door.

He killed the hot water and scrambled for a towel. He tied that sucker around his hips with a vengeance, at least until he found out what she wanted.

"Yeah?" Jack opened the door, a rush of cool air blasting his skin as the steam escaped.

She stood in the hall, backlit by the glow of the night-light in the galley. Towel around her like a toga, she was using a smaller cloth to blot the wet hair clinging to her shoulders.

"Sorry to get you out of the shower." Her dark eyes did a slow trek south, lingering on the knot in the terry cloth at his hips before she lifted her gaze. Tongue darting out to wet her lips, she shivered. "I just wanted to see if you had a robe. Or if you thought Keith would have one somewhere. I'm freezing."

Okay. A, she would wear something of his brother's over Jack's cold, dead body. And B, he had about a thousand other ideas for how to warm her up.

Neither of which he mentioned.

"Let me see." He stalked past her into the berth, where she'd slept the night before. The sheets were still rumpled from where she'd lain—and where he'd lain with her all too briefly.

Making a quick show of checking the wardrobe, Jack barely registered what was in there. He didn't want to see her in another man's threads.

"I'm surprised the hot tub didn't take the chill off." He found a wool blanket in a chest at the end of the bed and shook it out. It smelled like cedar, but it was clean. Warm.

"At first, it did. But when I got out to get my towel, I turned cold all over again even though the rain had stopped." She blinked up at him as he leaned closer to wrap the dark wool around her shoulders.

Only then did he notice the spaghetti straps were gone from her shoulders. No straps meant no tank top.

Just as he'd suggested, she must have gotten naked after he left. And didn't that realization freeze all brain function in a heartbeat? One minute, he was thinking semi-rationally. The next—bam, no gray-matter activity. He paused in the middle of wrapping her up.

"What's the matter?" She looked down at herself, probably trying to follow his gaze. "Is my towel still on?"

Her half smile was his first cue that she was messing with him. Teasing him when he was set to implode.

"Not for long if you don't back away." He told his hands to release the blanket, but they kept a tight grip on the hem where he held it, just above her breasts.

"It's not me who keeps running from this." She remained utterly still, not moving toward him. Not sprinting for the stairs.

"You had the bright idea of no kissing on this trip," he reminded her.

"So don't kiss me."

He studied her for the space of two heartbeats, waiting to make sure his sex-crazy brain hadn't misunderstood. But when she was still standing there, her damp body mere inches from his, he comprehended what she wanted all too clearly.

"Not a chance, Ally." He lowered his mouth to hers

and tasted her lips. "Some rules were meant to be broken."

Her neck arched back, her face tipped up to his as she let out a ragged little sigh. The taste of her went to his head like a straight shot, drugging him with sweetly addictive pleasure. Tightening his hold on the blanket around her, he tugged her nearer until she stumbled against him, never breaking the kiss.

The feel of her—warm and willing—stoked a fire at the base of his spine, sending flames licking upward. The need to be inside her flared hot and fast, a primal hunger he didn't understand. Already, this didn't feel like a one-time thing, not with his blood pounding in his ears and his fingers hooking inside her towel to loosen the knot. But he couldn't slow himself down. Not now.

"Did you really get naked out there?" he asked, fumbling with the fabric as he walked her backward toward the unmade bed.

"See for yourself," she urged, her hands running down his chest to the twitching muscles of his abs.

Then the terry cloth fell away, leaving them both naked except for the blanket he'd wrapped around her. She felt so good all at once that he could hardly take in all the places that teased his senses—her thigh against his, her breast flattened to his chest, her hips cradling a throbbing erection.

"Please say you thought about me when you took your clothes off." He hooked an arm beneath her legs and swept her up before depositing her on the bed.

From the hallway, the night-light spilled a green glow

on her perfect skin. She looked so good he was afraid he dreamed her, so he made quick work of joining her there. Feeling her warm and damp against him helped make the moment more real.

"I wished it was your hands peeling off my top," she assured him, miming the act of rolling a strap down one arm.

He smoothed one palm up her spine, arching her back so that her breast met his lips. He licked the tight peak and drew it into his mouth, suckling her until her fingernails dug into his shoulder. The scents of salt water and flowery soap teased his nostrils.

"I would have tasted every inch of you." The memory of her had followed him halfway around the world. He'd awoken some nights sweating and aching, dreaming about his mouth on her.

Just thinking about it sent his lips down the valley of her cleavage to her flat stomach. The gentle curve of her hip.

"I would have flown apart long before you covered every inch." Her husky words were breathless as she skimmed her fingers down his forearms. "Just getting naked had me twitchy and ready to come out of my skin."

Pausing in his descent, he looked up to meet her gaze in the half-light.

"But you saved that for me?" The slow thud of his heart seemed to echo inside of his chest.

Her skin was pale and perfect, her breasts taut and

upturned, as if waiting for his kiss. She levered herself up on one elbow.

"You give better orgasms than any hot-tub jet."

The fire at the base of his spine morphed into an inferno. The need to possess her branded his skin and left his flesh smoking as he slid his hands down her hips to the curls covering her sex, a neat triangle between her thighs.

Sliding off the bed, he made a place for himself there, ducking a shoulder beneath one leg and cradling the other in his hand. He could hear her ragged breathing, knew she was close to the edge even before he closed in on her slick heat. But there was no stopping now until he got his fill of her.

She tensed at the first stroke of his tongue up the heated center of her. Two strokes later and she writhed in the sheets, twisting the fabric in her fists as she fought off the inevitable. A growl shuddered through him, vibrating over his lips and humming against her skin as he worked her.

Her body arched up off the bed and she cried out, her fingers clamping around his wrists as if to hold him there. As if he had any intention of leaving. He steadied her in the aftermath, easing off just enough to give her time to catch her breath before he started all over again.

Once, twice, three times she found release that way. He didn't remember her being so exquisitely sensitive, her body so attuned to his every touch. The knowledge that he could do that to her rocked him to the core.

"Come inside me," she whispered, lifting herself up to tug on his shoulders and pull him closer. "I need you."

The raw want in her voice almost made him forget why he needed to hold back.

"I have no condoms. Nothing to protect you." He hadn't known she'd be on board the boat. Hell, he never expected they could smooth over the past long enough to share this again, even on a short-term basis.

He kissed his way up her body until he lay on the bed beside her, careful not to get too close, or he might lose all control.

"Are we too smart to trust the withdrawal method?" She splayed a palm across his chest, her calf muscle running lightly up his.

"I sure as hell hope so." Although in his condition, he didn't trust himself for long.

"Check the bathroom." She pointed to the half-open door with a jerk of her thumb. "It's the corporate party boat, right? Someone must have gotten busy on it before. There could be a half box stashed in a medicine cabinet."

Crazy as the idea sounded, he leaped to his feet and shoved open the door to the head.

"Nothing." Damn it. Unlike him, Keith hadn't been stuck on a destroyer for the better part of the last four years. Shouldn't his sex life warrant more than this?

On impulse Jack tugged open a drawer near the bed that functioned as a nightstand. And, hello, foil packets.

"Bingo." He held up a row of five for her to see. "And they aren't even expired."

She met his gaze in the dim light, her brown eyes glittering with mischief.

"Guess you have no excuses, Murphy." Reaching up, she tore off one packet and set it beside him on the bed. "You're all mine now. At least for tonight and four more times."

She grinned as she rolled her hips against him in flirtatious invitation, but he couldn't help reading between the lines. *Tonight and four more times.* The words underscored the time limit imposed by her relocation to Bar Harbor—a time limit that hovered tangibly between them. Tossing aside the extra condoms, he planned to make every encounter with Alicia something she'd never forget.

A SHADOW HAD PASSED through Jack's eyes. Alicia could see it clearly, since a moonbeam peeking through the clouds spilled over his face and onto one shoulder.

But as soon as it appeared, his expression cleared again, his gaze lit with a fire from within. For her. She wrapped her arms around his neck and drew him down, wanting to feel every ounce of him stretched out over her. Inside her.

She coiled a leg around his and rocked her hips against him. And while she'd meant the action to spur him on, she nearly sent herself hurtling over the edge again. Her whole body sparked into flame every time he got near, making her wonder if he'd hypnotized her four years ago. How else could she respond like Pavlov's dog to just a simple stroke of his finger?

His tongue?

"Ohhh." A moan rumbled up her throat as she realized how close she was all over again. How had he held back while she orgasmed like there was no tomorrow? "Hurry."

He sheathed himself with the condom she'd set out, his hands nudging her belly and her thigh while he worked with the prophylactic. She braved a peek at him, her gaze eating up the rippled ab muscles as he positioned himself between her thighs.

Flashbacks to other times together flitted through her brain for a moment, but she closed her eyes to shut them out, not wanting to spoil this chance to be with him just for the pleasure of it. She'd fallen hard for him once, and that was more than enough, thank you very much. This time, she'd take all the sensual bliss, all the sizzle, without the heartache.

"Open," he whispered, his breath warm against her skin as he brushed a kiss over her temple.

She inhaled deeply and edged one thigh higher as the hard, thick length of him slid over her core.

"Your eyes," he clarified, kissing the closed lids. "Open them. Look at me."

As she met his gaze, he edged inside her in perfect synchronization, so that by the time she'd dragged her lids all the way open, he was seated deep within her. He cupped her hip in one hand and cradled her jaw in the other, tipping her face to his. Her heart beat wildly, erratically, and she knew it wasn't because of how good he felt inside her.

It was because opening her eyes felt like opening her heart, if only for a moment.

Slamming her lids shut again, she closed out everything but the feeling. That much she could have. That much she would take.

Jack let go of her cheek to bracket her shoulders, his fists on either side of her on the mattress as he found a rhythm that pleased them both. Too soon, the pleasure built all over again, rolling through her like a tidal wave, pulling her under as the release pulsed along her feminine muscles. Dimly, she felt him find his own satisfaction, and she wished she'd contributed more to help take him to that place.

Still, his shout of satisfaction reverberated through her, reassuring her that he'd been right there with her in those final moments.

At last, sated and boneless, she stirred up just enough energy to tug him down onto the bed beside her. His scent was as familiar as the feeling of being wrapped in his arms. She rubbed her cheek along his chest, savoring the warmth of his skin and the silky dark hair at the center of his pecs. For a few more days, she would soak up all she could of him. Or at least, all she could without allowing her heart to get tangled up in the mix.

Jack Murphy had never wanted all she'd been ready to give him. So now she would dole out only this one small piece—the sexual side of her that he'd coaxed to life for the first time with his own two hands. Was it any wonder she fit so well with him when he'd been the man to take her virginity?

This time, she would simply enjoy what he had to offer. And when the day came to say goodbye in Maine, she would be the one to do the walking.

5

JACK HAD BEEN IN THE military long enough to know a battle line when he saw one. And Alicia had drawn hers clearly for him the night before when she'd closed her eyes and shut him out, broadcasting her intent to keep him at arm's length even when he was buried heart-deep inside her.

While he wasn't surprised, per se, he'd been…rattled. Okay, maybe a little stung. For four years, he'd remembered her the way she'd been when he'd left for officer candidate school in Newport. Back then, Alicia had been crazy about him, wearing her heart on her sleeve as she'd pulled him into her world. There was a coolness about her now that he imagined came from more maturity, at least in part. But he mourned the loss of that effusive, affectionate woman she'd been.

He watched her out of the corner of his eye the next afternoon as she sat on the forward deck, soaking in the late-summer sun while she worked on more notes for the bed-and-breakfast she planned to buy. That damn inn of hers. This morning, she'd shown him half-a-dozen photos and diagrams of the place. She had layouts of the existing structure with overlays of the additions and changes she wanted to make in five years and ten years.

What could he say when he'd been floored by her meticulous planning? Obviously, the place in Bar Harbor was about more than escaping him and Chatham. She truly had big plans for this project. But it was tough to share the enthusiasm when he thought she should open an inn back home where she had family to watch over her. Where he could be sure she didn't run into any trouble.

"Do you think we've reached the coast of Maine yet?" she asked him suddenly.

She shaded her eyes with one hand to study the green hills and beaches on the shore. Her hair bobbed in a loose knot at the back of her head, a few stray pieces escaping because of the constant breeze.

"No. We got a late start this morning, remember?" He checked the horizon for oncoming boats and set the self-steering mechanism so he could join her on the forward deck.

They'd showered together upon waking, an activity that had further depleted the condom resources and caused them to linger in bed for over an hour afterward. While Alicia had been as sweetly responsive physically as she had been the night before, she also held something back from him. If he didn't know her so well, he probably wouldn't have recognized it.

"I remember." She grinned at him over the sketch pad. "Are you fishing for compliments on another stellar performance?"

Dropping onto a seat cushion beside her, he tugged the paper from her hands and set it aside, weighing it down with a heavy picture book about Bar Harbor so her work wouldn't blow away.

"Hardly. But if your recall is faulty, I'm more than happy to refresh your memory." He figured his odds of bringing her back home to Massachusetts with him increased each time he undressed her.

They hadn't discussed what the night before meant, and he wasn't eager to press her for a commitment. Yet. But being with her again made him realize that's what he was aiming for.

For now, he would concentrate on taking down her barriers whenever he wasn't taking *her*. He trailed a finger down her arm, her skin sun-warmed through the gauzy white blouse she wore over a turquoise-colored tank top. Her denim cutoffs were so short the pockets peeked out from the frayed edges, displaying lean, tanned legs tucked underneath her on the seat.

"Your generosity knows no bounds." Unfurling her legs, she stretched out in the sun. "But since we're falling behind, I wonder if we should move out deeper into the ocean. We could make better time."

He let go of her shirt, sensing a battle of wills brewing.

"Safer for us if we hug the coast." Why take chances

with her? "It's a big, unwieldy boat for one person. We might as well take it easy and arrive in one piece."

She frowned. "You weren't concerned about the size of the boat that first night when I woke up in the middle of the Atlantic."

"I didn't know you were on board."

"So you'll take chances with yourself, but not with me."

"That's about the size of it."

Folding her arms across her midsection, she stared hard at the coastline, a furrow in her brow. "I can't imagine how you got the mistaken impression that I'm some fragile flower—"

"I don't think—"

"—because I can't picture many of your other girl-friends playing football with your brothers." She cast him a dark look, the wind catching tendrils that escaped the knot in her hair. "Or personalizing a weight-lifting program to maximize power on the breast stroke. Oh, and were you aware that I am *certified* to *teach water sports?*"

"Then I'm sure you're familiar with survival statistics for capsized crafts with visibility of the coast versus those that are out to sea." He wouldn't budge on this point.

"Didn't we agree to share steering on this boat?" she reminded him. "That means I can weigh in on decisions about the voyage."

"With the understanding that, as captain, I reserve the right to pull rank when necessary."

"You realize you run the risk of me jumping overboard to swim ashore if I think I'm going to be even a moment late for my appointment with the owner of the bed-and-breakfast?"

Something in her voice warned him she wasn't kidding.

"This isn't the *Vesta,* Ally. It's one thing to sail in a boat you know inside and out. But I'd never been on this tank until two nights ago." He slapped a palm against the decking around the hot tub. "I don't know how it reacts in a storm or big swells, so why push our luck? Besides, we've got plenty of time to get there."

"You're not just delaying, to try and talk me out of buying the bed-and-breakfast?"

If anything, he would have delayed to spend more time with her before she hightailed it out of his life for good. But that didn't take away from his primary reason for hugging the coastline.

"You're really jazzed about this place, aren't you?" He reached behind her to retrieve the notebook she'd laid aside, checking the horizon for water traffic before returning his attention to the diagrams and lists she'd made.

"I've worked hard to afford something that's all mine." She peered over his shoulder at the main drawing of the inn, as if she couldn't see it often enough. "I really thought Keith would help me finalize the business plan on this trip. That's the reason I agreed to let him take me to Bar Harbor."

If Jack had had that kind of enthusiasm for his

father's resort complex, he'd still be a part of the family company.

"I never knew it was so important to you to start your own business." He turned toward her, reassessing her yet again.

"Turns out there was a *lot* we didn't know about each other." She met his gaze and he could see the wheels spinning behind those pretty brown eyes. "For instance, I had no idea you harbored a deep-seated need to serve in the military. When we used to talk about a future, it never came up."

Ah, crap.

Words escaped him. He should have known she'd bring it up sooner or later, but he hadn't considered what—or how much—to say.

He must have taken too long to decide because she turned away again, her eyes fixed on the shore. "Never mind. There are some mysteries destined to remain in the cold-case file, I guess. Your need to serve your country seemingly overnight will have to be one of them."

Overnight? Hell, it hadn't felt that way to him. But then, he'd tried to keep that part of his life away from Alicia to protect her. Maybe that had been a mistake. One thing was for sure. If he continued to keep his secrets, he'd have no chance of talking her into coming back home with him.

FURIOUS AT HERSELF for asking Jack about the past, Alicia shaded in her latest sketch a little too hard, digging into the paper with the pencil instead of darkening the roof of a converted carriage house she hoped to repurpose into a honeymoon suite for her guests.

Hadn't she told herself that she was going to keep things simple with him this week? But no. She had dared to ask Mr. Closed Mouth about his navy stint, and had felt him raise his shields as if he were the *USS Enterprise*.

"Remember when the terrorist group claimed responsibility for kidnapping those two female journalists? It was around Valentine's Day the year I enlisted." Jack's voice seemed to be speaking a different language for a minute as her mind grappled with the fact that he was actually sharing something with her.

Slowly, she put down her pencil.

"Christina Marcel and her camerawoman." Alicia remembered the two of them perfectly. The war in Iraq had been at a low point, with casualties in the news every day. Even abroad, there had been incidents, with different groups claiming retaliation against the U.S. for their role in the fighting. "Christina wasn't that much older than me."

The news had been all over campus at Boston College. The journalists were from New York, but they'd worked for a station that broadcast to the Boston area. Marcel and her colleague had been held six weeks before being let go. But at the time, many other prisoners had been brutalized and killed, often in front of rolling cameras, to the horror of their families back home.

"Christina is our cousin." Jack's green eyes were haunted and murky.

The pencil rolled off the sketch pad and onto the deck while Alicia tried to absorb the news.

"What do you mean? How?" The questions didn't make sense, but neither did what he was saying. He was related to that woman and had never told her?

The whole country had been glued to their televisions as they worried about the kidnapped journalists. Why wouldn't he mention a connection?

"My mother is from an extremely wealthy New York family. Most people don't know her background because she eloped with a poor kid from Brooklyn and her family disowned her." Jack flexed his fingers before fisting them. He leaned forward, propping his elbows on his knees. "Plus, Christina doesn't share her dad's name, since her mom didn't marry her father. Anyway, it's not common knowledge that she's related to a wealthy family—not her New York clan nor her relationship to the Murphys. We were advised to keep that connection a secret, since her captors might have increased their demands if they'd known about us. Not that we wouldn't have paid, far from it. But the government advised us not to let it be known that she was potentially a very valuable prisoner."

Alicia's mind reeled with the picture she was beginning to form. Jack's family had been a part of some international horror and she hadn't even been aware of it. His thoughts had been on a kidnapped girl overseas while she'd been whining that he'd missed another one of her swim meets.

"Your family kept it a secret." It wasn't just Jack who'd withheld the information then. His whole family had been trying to comply with a hostage negotiation. "I wish I'd known," Alicia said softly. Then once again realized that was probably the selfish thing to say. "That is, I would have been more supportive. All those trips overseas for your father's business…"

"Some of them were for business, but several were to meet with people we thought might be able to help free Christina. Traveling for the company was an easy cover and my brothers and I took turns trying to urge various businesses and governments to get involved with demanding her release. We tried to keep it low-key so no one realized our personal interest. But almost right away, my brother Daniel decided to put on a uniform and go make peace the old-fashioned way."

Jack stood and moved toward the helm to make a few adjustments to their course. Alicia used the time to peer around at the quiet, calm water. Her insides were anything but.

"He convinced you to join, too?" She tried to remember what she and Jack had talked about during those months when he'd had all of this weighing on his heart.

And while she regretted not being more supportive during such a trying time, she couldn't help a stab of resentment that he hadn't trusted her with any of it. She'd felt like part of his family. But she hadn't been allowed into the fold with the most important Murphy affairs.

"No. He never asked me to join. You know what a rebel he is. He just made the decision and never looked back. But while Ryan was off learning the family business, from the inside out, my part in Murphy Resorts was smaller and I didn't enter the business until a few years after him. So I was the stand-in oldest brother for a long time. Maybe that's why it felt wrong to watch Danny go to war while I—"

"Stayed home and went to my spring formal." Alicia shook her head, the last few strands coming loose from the twist in her hair. "No wonder my world seemed so juvenile to you."

She'd just qualified for the women's National Collegiate Athletic Association swim championship in three events that year. She'd been a junior captain on a team full of promising talent. But damn it, she would have been more understanding about Jack's decision if he'd given her any inkling of what had been going on in his world. After finger combing a few snarls from her wind-tousled hair, she tied it into a low ponytail.

"Never." He didn't return to the foredeck, remaining in the captain's chair. "I looked forward to being with you and not thinking about what was going on in the family. Christina's capture stirred up a lot of old resentments between my dad and my mother's family. Chrissy's mother was the only one my mom had any contact with—we'd met her family a few times. And my mother was stressed because her efforts to reach out to the rest of the relatives were rebuffed. Then Danny..."

"What?" She knew the least about Daniel Murphy. She'd gotten to know the patriarch, Robert, and his oldest son, Ryan, through her internship with Murphy Resorts. In high school she'd been in the same class as Kyle and Axel, so she'd witnessed their rise to hockey stardom in college and then in the NHL. Keith had been so friendly at family gatherings that he'd been easy to get to know. And of course, she'd fallen head over heels for Jack.

But Danny Murphy remained a mystery other than his stint with a rock band that had gone on to achieve fame and fortune without him. Also, that he'd taken a navy contract the same day Jack had.

"He was crazy about Christina's journalist friend, the camerawoman who was taken in the kidnapping."

Alicia tried to process what that meant. "He didn't think he'd...save her?"

Both hostages had been returned safely six weeks after they'd been taken. But no doubt those weeks would have been harrowing for someone close to the captives.

"No. If anything, we knew we'd be farther from the negotiations if we entered the service, but Danny was going nuts thinking he wasn't doing enough." Jack scrubbed a hand through his dark hair, his gaze a million miles away even though he stared at a yacht cruising out to sea just ahead of them. "He said he'd always felt called to serve, and if he didn't answer the call then, he'd never get out from under the family business to make it happen."

She could see that argument resonating with the younger man Jack had been.

"And you realized you felt the same way."

His eyes cleared, narrowing on her. "How did you know?"

She shrugged, unable to remember the exact conversations they'd had that made all this make sense for her. But somehow she'd always known that Jack had never felt comfortable with a life of wealth and privilege.

"Any other guy your age would have been over the moon to make all those trips to Europe on a company credit card, but you'd call me at midnight from a glitzy hotel, jet-lagged and cranky." Her heart ached a little at the memory of hour-long conversations. Phone sex that left them both breathless and hungry to be together for real. "It doesn't surprise me that you would appreciate the sense of purpose the military could give you. I just wish you had let me share that side of it, instead of making me think you'd ditched me because I was too young and superficial for you to share something so monumental in your life."

She was exaggerating the case, since he'd never come out and expressed it that way. But when he didn't contradict her long-imagined explanation for his disappearance from her life, queasiness churned in her belly. Rising, she left the forward deck to join him at the helm, her eyes never leaving his face.

"You truly *did* think I was too young and superficial."

"Not superficial." He tugged the wheel to the right to avoid another boat's wake. "But you can't deny we were at different points in our lives. You didn't need to shoulder all my worries with the family when you were dealing with your father. Remember? The hostage situation took place when he was trying to get you to transfer to Harvard—"

"I remember. The master manipulator knew what was best for me, even though I was having the best season of my career. Of course, swimming never meant anything to him." She shook her head, her heart full of so much regret and sadness that she didn't know where to put it all. "And while my father decided what was best for me academically, you decided what was best for our relationship, without consulting me. You never considered letting me in, to share the things what were closest to your heart."

"I did consider it." He didn't elaborate, however.

Perhaps because they both knew he'd considered it only until he nixed the idea.

"But ultimately, you decided to let me worry about Harvard and my future in swimming while you shouldered the bigger concerns on your own." Frustration simmered and she wasn't sure how to keep a lid on it. Heat built behind her eyes in direct proportion to the hurt and resentment. "Did it ever occur to you that I shared what was going on between my dad and me because I cared about a future with you? I cared about your opinion. You, on the other hand, didn't care about mine."

She couldn't tell if she felt better or worse after their heart-to-heart. While it helped to understand more of what Jack had been going through four years ago, it stung to realize how completely he'd shut her out back then. She'd loved him and he'd…enjoyed the escapism their relationship offered.

The heat of frustration steamed over her skin until her neck itched, and her cheeks flushed with mortification as she realized she'd never really known this man at all.

"I didn't say that."

Of course, he didn't clarify anything, either. She couldn't bear one more minute of Jack Murphy's brand of the cold shoulder. Why had she thought the night before meant anything to him? But that was her fault. She should have asked these questions *before* last night's brilliant plan for seduction.

"Would you mind killing the engine?" She headed for the swim platform at the back of the boat.

"What are you doing?" He rose to follow her, but she could hear he'd hit the off switch first.

The engine stopped and she watched the wake behind the boat to be sure the propeller went still.

"I'm going swimming," she announced, pulling off her shirt and stepping out of her shorts to reveal another tankini top and matching swim-shorts set. This one was turquoise with sleek, no-nonsense straps.

"You can't swim here." He peered around, clearly trying to find some evidence to back up his statement.

But since there were no other boats, no skiers and no

Jaws-style fins sticking out of the water, he was plain out of luck.

"Don't be ridiculous. I'm hot and mad. I'm also young and impetuous, part of the reason you ditched me four years ago, remember?" She pointed to the water. "The propeller is still. The engine is off. There are no swirls to suggest a strong current. So with any luck, I'll reach the shore before dark."

She wasn't serious. She just needed to cool off, needed a moment to herself. To indulge in something that never failed to bring her peace.

But that didn't stop her from enjoying the priceless expression on his face just before she stepped off the platform and into the Atlantic.

6

CHASE AFTER ALICIA? Or ensure his brother's splashy yacht didn't float out to sea without them?

With a curse, Jack moved back to the helm to hit the switch for dropping the anchor, after he was certain Alicia was nowhere near the line. She bobbed and floated a few yards off the port side, looking more like a dolphin at play than a woman hell-bent on getting to shore. Getting away from him.

She couldn't have been serious about swimming to the coast. She knew better than to try something so dangerous with boat traffic and unfamiliar water all around her. Still, she'd given him a hell of a scare.

"I don't see why you're mad at me," he called down to her as he tossed a life ring tied to a long line into the water for safety's sake.

"That's because you don't understand me even one little bit," she retorted, her golden hair sopping and dark where it was plastered to her head. Her freckles stood out on her skin, which looked paler than usual.

No doubt she was cold. The Atlantic in the Northeast never turned all that warm in summer. And the water was deep here. Still, she kicked into a back float as if she had all the time in the world to taunt him from the sea's rippling surface.

He tried to remember how much her antics irritated him, instead of noticing her killer legs. Her fearless willingness to back up the smack she talked. Hell, she could be sixty years old and she'd still be young at heart. That was just the kind of personality she had.

"If I take the boat a little farther out to sea and make better time tonight, will you come back aboard and explain it to me so I do understand?"

She bit her lip, thinking about it, apparently. In the meantime, he heard the signal that meant the anchor had hit bottom. If he wanted it to set properly, he'd have to start the engine and pull forward against the line— something he wouldn't do with Alicia in the water.

"You can be difficult to talk to," she protested. "You're very stubborn."

"Says the woman who jumped overboard because she was miffed."

Peering over her shoulder, she lifted a dripping hand out of the water to shield her eyes as she gazed at the shore.

"It really isn't that far…."

Temper and impatience threatened to get the best of him. "If I have to come in there to retrieve you—"

"I'd give you a run for your money and you know it." She smiled beatifically. "But I'll spare you the trouble, since you've promised to pick up the pace on the journey."

She swam toward the boat, her lean, toned limbs propelling her quickly now that she'd made up her mind. Just seeing her handle herself in the water—from her swim form to the way she hoisted herself onto the platform with ease—made him realize he didn't need to worry about taking her farther from the coast. She'd grown up on the water, same as him. She was a strong swimmer. And she was smart about boats.

How many other ways had he underestimated her over the years?

The thought faded from his mind as she stood at the rear of the craft, her striped swimsuit suspending all his cognitive activity. The skimpy fabric molded to perfect curves as if it enjoyed the feel of her and couldn't get enough. Just like him.

Holy. Hell.

He'd just slept with her the night before, but it felt like light years since he'd touched her.

"Umm...towel?" She glanced around the boat while seawater sluiced down her body to pool at her feet.

With an effort, he forced himself to move, to head down the stairs to the cabin below, where he retrieved a roll of blue terry cloth from his brother's well-stocked cabinet. Shaking it out, he jogged back up the steps and wrapped it around Alicia's shoulders.

"You ought to do something about that temper," he scolded gruffly, in an effort not to leer.

"I did," she reminded him, unrepentant, as she bent

to dry off long, slender legs. Her hair dripped on the deck beside her arched foot. "The swim cooled things off in a hurry."

"Is that what you're going to do when your guests at the bed-and-breakfast start getting on your nerves? There's not always a boat to jump off, you know." His eyes lingered on the swell of her breasts, the damp fabric of her swimsuit looking as if it wasn't up to the task of restraining her.

"Funny, no one's ever ticked me off enough to make me *want* to dive into the Atlantic before. I think my guests will be safe enough."

Unlike her breasts, which were about to come under siege by his fingers if he didn't find something else to do besides stare in hunger.

With an effort, he turned on his heel to take his seat at the helm and pull in the anchor. He wished there was a way to pull in his libido as quickly.

"You mean to tell me, of the people who get under your skin, I'm in a class by myself?" He hit the necessary buttons to retract the anchor line, and checked his gauges. "We've butted heads enough times that I always pictured you as having a temper."

From his peripheral vision, he could see her wrap up in the towel again.

"Only where you're concerned." She padded along the deck, her bare feet silent on the hardwood. "No one else has ever walked away from me without a backward glance. I'm sure that makes me a little more sensitive around you than I am with most people."

Bending, she peered over his shoulder to study the fish finder, a sonar readout of shapes beneath the surface that helped locate different kinds of sea life.

"You're never going to forgive me for that, are you?" Maybe he hadn't fully appreciated how much his defection had hurt her.

He'd always pictured her moving on soon after, dating other guys and immersing herself in swim competitions.

"I will forgive you. But I have to confess it will be hard to forget about it." Gently, she swatted his arm with the damp end of the towel as she stood beside him. "You went on to pursue your life and I chose my own path. That's fine. But it's strange to be here with you now after going for so long without a word. And it's really, really strange to think how fast I could fall back into bed with you when I...probably shouldn't."

He had to bite his tongue to keep from telling her there was no going back now. And to keep from kissing her senseless to reinforce the message. Because that would be a caveman thing to do.

Still, when he turned to look at her—really look at *her,* not just her smoking hot body and her competitive, take-on-the-world demeanor—his throat closed up so tight he couldn't speak if he tried. She was being honest and forthright with him, while he...didn't have a damn clue what he expected from this completely unanticipated window of time with her. All he knew was that he wanted another chance to explore the attraction.

Dark eyes swept over him, warm and probing,

searching for answers he didn't have. He might have acted on the tension between them and kissed her except that an annoying ringing noise sounded a few inches away. Again. And again.

"Um…" Alicia reached around him, her touch breaking through his thoughts more than the electronic chirping. "It sounds like your cell phone."

She came up with the device a moment later, just in time for him to accept the incoming call.

"Hello?" He hadn't even checked the caller ID, since he'd been lost in thought about Alicia.

His gaze followed her as she turned to give him privacy. Dragging the towel along with her, she stepped up to the foredeck near the hot tub and tipped her face to the sun.

"Jack!" his father barked into the phone. "Is that you?"

"Hi, Dad." He wished now that he'd screened the call, since he had no intention of sitting still for one of the old man's lectures when he didn't want to waste a second of his time with Alicia. To hear his father talk, Robert Murphy had all the answers and could straighten out any of his kids' lives if given half a chance. His latest brainstorm involved getting Jack back on the family payroll. "Look, I'm about to lose cell service out on the boat—"

"Jack, I'd really like you to stop by the office when you get back. You've been home for four weeks and we really need—"

"I'm going to stop you right there." He had no desire

to hear a lecture about his need to commit to Murphy Resorts. "I appreciate the opportunities you've given me, Dad. But I've got a different future in mind."

Nearby, Alicia busied herself with her notes on the bed-and-breakfast to give him some space.

"And I'm interested to hear about that future. Why don't you come in on Friday and we'll talk about it?" his father pressed.

Jack loved his family. Really, he did. But the Murphy clan was too close sometimes, with everyone offering an opinion on what you should do, shouldn't do, and why they knew better than you. He had an MBA and a successful navy career under his belt. Didn't that give anyone some reassurance that he'd be able to figure out where to go next without screwing up his life?

"We'll talk soon, Dad," he agreed for expediency's sake. "Tell Mom she did a great job with the party." Winding up their conversation with another promise to be in touch, he disconnected the call.

His eyes moved back to Alicia, busily trying to stay out of his way as she flipped through her papers. He didn't mean to exclude her anymore, not after how upset she'd been at being shut out of his family's scare with Christina. He'd been so focused on not upsetting her back then—not foisting off his problems—that he'd walled her out of the drama completely. And maybe she would have been a comfort to his parents as much as to him.

Jack would make her forget about the long-ago

mistakes he'd made while they were dating, and start thinking about him as a prospect for her future.

But first he needed to make sure she stayed in Chatham, close enough for him to resurrect the toe-curling chemistry that sizzled every time they touched.

"Is EVERYTHING OKAY back home?" Alicia couldn't help but ask after she'd noticed Jack had finished his call.

She'd always liked the Murphy clan. The family might feel crowded by the big personality of their brash business-mogul father. But Alicia appreciated the way he kept an eye on everyone, occasionally pulling in outsiders and making them feel like family, too. Jack's parents had both traveled to one of her swim meets when neither her father nor brother had bothered to attend a single competition.

If things had been different between her and Jack, Alicia would have gotten more than a sexy, warm-hearted guy in the bargain. She would have inherited a great family, too.

"Things are fine. My father has been hounding me to return to Murphy Resorts, but working in the family fold just isn't for me." Jack started the engine again and flipped a few buttons to bring the craft to life.

"No?" She knew he hadn't loved all the travel involved in his work managing the global properties division, but he'd been very good at his job.

"It's not a career I would have chosen for myself, and there are plenty of other people to fill my shoes." The vessel crept forward while he plotted a new course.

Once they were under way again—headed deeper out to sea—Jack came up to the deck where she sat.

"I don't think you're easily replaced," she argued, knowing how hard Jack worked.

"Actually, *you'd* be great at my old job," he continued, green eyes lighting with the fire of a new idea. "I don't know why you didn't apply for a position with the company after your internship. The freelance work you did with the golf tournament was first rate."

She shook her head, wondering if he had any idea how much he took after his father.

"First of all, I really think things are going to come together for me in Bar Harbor. But even if they don't, working for your family might create a sticky situation for us down the road." She tucked her notebook under her thigh to keep her papers from blowing away as the boat picked up speed. Her movement caused her shoulder to brush against his, sending an electric pulse all the way down her arm. "While last night was fun, I didn't get the impression it was headed anywhere serious."

His diplomatic silence of one long minute seemed to confirm as much.

Reminding her why she would have to view this time on the boat as a fun diversion only.

"It wouldn't be awkward for us, because I'm not ever going back to work for my father," he said finally, tackling a completely different part of her concern.

The lean muscle of his upper arm grazed hers, sparking memories of all that warm strength wrapped around her body the night before. How could a man and woman fit together so perfectly when it came to the physical part of a relationship, yet fail each other so badly on a deeper level? And yes, she'd decided she must have fallen short in their past relationship if he'd kept her in the dark about his cousin. Maybe she'd been too wrapped up in her independence, her own family and pursuing her swimming ambitions to see what was really going on with Jack.

She regretted not being there for him when he needed her.

"So why aren't you returning to the family business?"

"I like having a sense of purpose in my professional life that stretches beyond raking in the big bucks."

"Your dad is hardly some greedy corporate shark."

"But he's definitely profit driven." Peering around the horizon for traffic on the water, Jack got to his feet. "The big house on the Cape and the jet-setting across Europe was never my style."

He waved for her to join him at the helm, obviously wanting to stick close to the controls until they were out of the more popular boating lanes.

"I remember you said the same thing about buying the *Vesta*." He'd purchased it on eBay for a song, and spent a summer restoring it. He'd been working on it before they started dating, but he hadn't finished it— and christened it—until after they were an item.

Those hot August days when she'd come over to the house to hang out with Kyle and his friends were etched in her brain with visions of Jack hand-sanding the hull of the sailboat. She remembered tanned, glistening muscles sprinkled with a sheen of sawdust.

And she'd been dying for him to notice her.

"Right." He slid into the captain's chair as he gave a nod to a guy on an aluminum fishing trawler. "I didn't want the big-ass boat my dad had his eye on for me. I wanted something proven seaworthy. A classic. And I wanted to buy it myself."

"You also bought it from a guy who was going to lose his house and needed to sell off everything." She hadn't thought about that for a long time, but it fit with the way Jack moved through his life—always helping out someone else. "Kind of like how you're investing in all these run-down bars? Are those club owners struggling, too?"

She twisted her damp hair into a knot on top of her head. Finding a lone golf tee rolling around in a tray of loose change near the windshield, she threaded the wooden object into the knot to hold it in place.

"I'm hardly the benefactor of bar owners. I just happen to like live music, and if those places go under, we'll have a lot fewer venues for cultivating new talent."

"A philanthropist with a taste for the blues." She shook her head, laughing at the image of him paying the bars to stay open so his favorite bands could play. "Seriously, Jack, if you're not going into the bar business and you're not working for your dad, what's next for you now that you're done floating around the Pacific?"

"You really want to know?"

"Yes."

"And I really want to know why *you* feel the need to move three states away to start a business."

Alicia frowned. She didn't have any intention of defending the move to Bar Harbor again. Besides, how could she tell him she couldn't bear to watch The One Who Got Away move on with the next girl? She hated to admit it to herself, let alone speak it out loud.

"Since I don't want to talk and neither do you, what do you say we play a game of poker for the answers?" He pulled out a deck of cards from the same change tray where she'd found the golf tee. "Loser has to answer the question of the winner's choosing."

Damn it. He knew she couldn't resist a challenge any more than he could.

"Since when are we counting poker as a legitimate form of competition?"

"Would you rather arm wrestle?" He flexed a biceps to emphasize his obvious advantage in that arena.

A suggestion that ticked her off even though the sight of his arms made her salivate most of the time.

"How about we fish for it?"

He scrubbed a hand along his jaw, considering. "Whoever catches the biggest fish gets to ask their question."

"Loser has to answer *and* cook the fish," she clarified, already seeing him at the on-board grill in her mind's eye.

"Deal. Care to up the stakes?" Something about the

mischievous wriggle of his eyebrows warned her that whatever he had in mind would be trouble.

It didn't mean she could say no.

"Name your terms, Murphy."

"Winner claims a sexual favor." His green eyes seared her as his gaze locked on her, and she had the distinct impression he already had something specific in mind.

Something he was visualizing right this moment.

A heat wave flashed along her skin. Her heart rate quadrupled. She had to lick her lips to edge words from a throat gone dry.

"You have yourself a deal."

7

HER COMPETITIVE NATURE had blinded her to the truth—
she'd never been much of a fisher.

In a bid to grab her father's attention at an early age,
she'd always been the first to volunteer and the first to
line up for a competition. She'd hoped a win would snag
her dad's notice. It hadn't, of course. But she'd found a
lot of other satisfaction in ambition. That's how she'd
discovered her talent for swimming.

Unfortunately, her race to enter a fishing contest with
Jack didn't seem destined to end favorably. Especially
not when he got a second bite on his line within a few
minutes.

"What is that?" she yelped, jumping to her feet as
his reel went spinning about a hundred miles an hour,
his line yanked tight.

"Something big. Crap." He scrambled to find lever-
age. "There's no harness for stand-up fishing."

"Put the rod in the holder!" She pointed to the gizmo

he'd showed her that secured the rod to the boat when wrestling a big catch.

Before he could, the reel stopped spinning as the line ran out. His arms were yanked forward, pitching his whole body off balance. She screamed as Jack skidded toward the edge of the deck, still holding the fishing rod.

"It's gotta be five hundred pounds." His voice was hoarse with the strain of holding on to the catch, but he managed a laugh even as the veins on his forehead bulged. "I bet it's a bluefin."

"Let it go!" She dropped her gear and ran to him, hooking a hand in the waistband of his cargo shorts.

As if she could hold back a two-hundred-pound guy and Shamu, too.

"Depends," he muttered between gritted teeth, his body slipping closer to the deck railing as he risked a glance at her. "Do I win?"

If she hadn't been scared to death for him, she might have let him go overboard with the damn fish. "Yes! For crying out loud, Jack—"

He hit something on the reel and the line spun free of the rod. The tension released so fast she stumbled backward with the jolt. The whole boat rocked as if freed of a giant anchor.

In the aftermath of the battle, the sea felt oddly calm and quiet. Gentle waves sloshed the hull as she and Jack each caught their breath.

He must have recovered his sooner because the next sound she heard was warm male laughter.

Blinking against the bright sun, she focused in on him where he sprawled on the deck, the fishing rod by his side as he propped himself up on one elbow. Watching her.

"You nearly got yourself killed, and scared me out of my mind," she reminded him sternly. "What, might I ask, is so amusing?"

"You should have seen your expression when you conceded the fight." His grin was so big now that the elusive second dimple—the one in his cheek—had put in an appearance.

She frowned harder than he smiled.

"I'm sure anger and disbelief isn't my most attractive look," she conceded.

His grin faded.

"It just goes to show you what lengths a guy will go to in order to be with you." Shoving aside the rod, he slid over on the deck until they sat beside each other, their backs resting against the built-in seats. "I was dying to win that bet."

"You *could have* died winning that damn bet," she admonished, although she was feeling less mad now that he sat so close to her, his hand slipping on top of hers. "You must really want to ask me a question."

"Yeah. But I have to confess I'm looking forward to the other aspect even more."

The sexual favor.

Awareness flamed hot between them. Her breath hitched in her throat and her mouth felt dry.

"So what's your question? You want to know more

about my move to Bar Harbor?" She let her head tip onto his shoulder, just for a moment, she told herself. Her heart rate hadn't quite recovered from seeing him wrestle the big fish.

If anything had happened to him…

Her heart lurched in her chest, revealing how much she still cared about him in spite of everything.

"No." His cheek rested on top of her head, the bristles at his jaw catching her hair. "I want to ask something stupid and selfish. Something I have no right to ask at all."

Surprised by the tension in his voice, she disentangled herself enough to look him in the eye.

"What?"

He stared down at the remote control that operated the GPS for the anchoring feature that kept the boat in position by satellite. Finally, he set it aside and met her gaze.

"What made you go out with Chase Freeman after we broke up?"

"Chase?" She tried to think why such a short chapter in her life would inspire the obvious jealousy she heard in his voice. "The banker?"

Jack rolled his eyes. "Or whatever he calls himself these days. Last I heard from him he was a Wall Street superstar."

"I forgot you two would have graduated the same year." In a small town, the dating options weren't exactly abundant. No matter that the seasonal population swelled to astronomical numbers. The year-round residents in Chatham were only so plentiful.

"Yeah? I'm willing to bet he didn't forget you were my ex-girlfriend." Jack picked up her hand and held it, smoothing his fingers over her knuckles in a way that gave her shivers despite the mild weather.

"I'm sensing an old rivalry here?"

"It's not a big deal." He shrugged his shoulders, even though they were still so taut and tense that the motion appeared decidedly awkward. "And it's none of my business, since we were broken up. I've just always wondered about it because it seemed so sudden. After I left for Rhode Island, you dated Chase and then Tom, one right after the other and…yeah. Why?"

Clamping her other hand on top of his roving one, she captured his palm between hers.

"You're right about it being none of your business. But since I can see it upset you, I'm going to confess I thought that getting back in the dating pool would help me shake the funk of you leaving." Memories of that summer were still painful. "My dad kept a close eye on me around then to personally ensure I didn't make the trip to Omaha for the Olympic-team trials in swimming. He staged some kind of weird intervention with a bunch of his Wall Street cronies the week before the trials, where they all gathered to inform me there was lots of money to be made in business and none in amateur sports. Basically, Dad wanted to be sure I knew my Olympic hopes were juvenile."

"Wow. I didn't know you were seriously considering

trying out. Why didn't you just leave? Get on a plane and fight for your dream?" Jack had always gotten along with Alicia's father, but maybe part of that stemmed from the fact that Bruce LeBlanc went out of his way to be affable with Jack.

"In retrospect, I wish I had. But I was tired of fighting about everything, and I was so exhausted I knew I wouldn't perform at my best level, anyhow. Maybe my father had gotten into my head a little more than I realized."

Jack raised his eyebrows but made no comment. Hating the personal-confession time, Alicia retrieved her fishing pole from where she'd dropped it, and slid toward the edge of the deck to recast.

"Dad was angry with me for giving up my job with Murphy Resorts. And he was even less impressed with me for 'losing' you. You can guess how well that went over."

"I'm still trying to process the fact that Bruce stifled a shot at the Olympics for his own daughter. What the hell was he thinking? Ally, I didn't mean to bring up—"

"It's okay. I was just getting to the point about Chase. But this is all relevant." Staring down into the fathomless Atlantic, she searched for fish and answers. It had been a long time since she'd thought about that crappy summer. "By the time I told my dad I'd had enough of his plans for my life, I was determined to put on a front of having it all together. And I figured I needed to get out of the house as much as possible to survive that last summer at home. So I threw myself into a new job as a water-sports instructor. I was at the beach every day and saw a lot of people, including Chase."

"I couldn't picture you being dazzled by the 'Wall Street superstar' routine." Jack sounded more accepting. Less jealous.

With good reason. She'd never lost her heart to anyone but him.

"We only went out a few times, since he turned out to be incredibly self-centered and a little too much like my dad's money-driven colleagues. But I needed a diversion. So when I broke up with him, I went out with Tom Rupert a few times. And a couple of other unmemorable guys over the next year." She felt her line tug and adjusted her grip on the rod. "I guess I threw myself into dating with as much ambition as I tackle most things. I didn't think about the fact that it might make me appear…undiscriminating."

She stood, welcoming the physical outlet of fishing, since she felt twitchy and uncomfortable with too much self-revelation.

"It didn't." Jack put on a glove and grabbed the line to steer it away from the engine's propeller. Even at a standstill, the blade could cut the heavy nylon if the pilot wasn't careful. "You had every reason to move on."

Because he'd already moved on with his life by that time.

Recalling as much didn't bolster her spirit, but at least she'd tackled the question. Been a good sport.

Reaching lower on the line, Jack jerked up her catch.

A long silver fish gleamed in the sun, which had shifted closer to the horizon.

"What is it?" She sincerely hoped he intended to help her clean it.

"Dinner." Grinning, he dropped a kiss on her cheek and removed the hook from the fish's mouth. "I'll go put this on ice so we can work on the more *interesting* part of our bet."

The sexual favor?

Her gaze flashed to his.

"You didn't think I'd forget, did you?"

The hot anticipation in his eyes burned through her. Distracted her completely. Gave her something heady to fantasize about as he moved to put away their rods and gear.

Because even though she'd been on the losing end of their bet, she had the feeling she would enjoy every moment of whatever he had in mind.

"YOU WANT ME TO WHAT?" Her eyes were wide as she hugged her arms around herself in the cooling breeze.

The sky had turned purple and pink in the west, the color lighting her skin with a warm glow.

It was a rare moment when Alicia LeBlanc didn't look completely sure of herself.

And it probably made Jack a total cad that he couldn't help but enjoy her uncertainty as she shifted from one foot to the other on the foredeck near the hot tub just before sunset.

"I want you to give up the reins. Let me have control."

He closed the distance between them now that he'd cleaned up the deck. Dinner could wait until after he'd cashed in on the prize he wanted most.

"While you do what, exactly?" She watched him warily, but her chest rose and fell with rapid breaths that told him she wasn't completely opposed to hearing him out.

"Whatever I like." He growled the words into her ear so she could feel how much he wanted this. Wanted *her* with no restraints.

"That isn't much of a favor," she protested, her fingers digging into the fabric of his shirt and knotting up in the cotton as she dragged herself closer. "Don't you want…"

She glanced south meaningfully.

His erection throbbed in response, clearly liking that idea just fine. But he planned on making this favor as much for her as for him. He had only so many days to convince her to give him a second chance.

"I'm saving that request for the next bet I win," he promised, threading his fingers through the belt loops of her cargo shorts and drawing her hips to his. "Tonight, I want to see you get in touch with your submissive side."

"I don't think I have one of those." She brushed a tantalizing kiss along his lips with slow deliberation. "Sorry."

She stared at him in the twilight, unapologetic in spite of her words.

"You think you can distract me with kisses?"

"Maybe." Arching into him, she pressed her breasts to his chest. "How am I doing?"

"A little too well," he admitted, his brain already seizing up at the feel of her. "That's why I'm going to stop you right there." He eased back about half an inch, which was all his fevered body could manage. "And demand you pay up your end of the bet."

Her frown came deliciously close to a pout, her lips pursed like a berry ready for squeezing.

"Submissive?" She shivered again and he decided it was time to warm her up.

Leaning down, he flipped the cover off the hot tub, releasing a cloud of steam into the rapidly cooling night air. They hadn't seen another boat in hours and were well out of the main traffic lanes, so he wasn't worried about witnesses.

"That's right. Total compliance. But don't worry, I'm not going to do anything too kinky. Yet."

Eyes narrowing, she lifted a hand to the hem of her shirt and whipped it up, over her head. Off.

Her pink cotton bra molded to subtle curves, her body visible in the fading light thanks to the glow from the illuminated tub. A silver-star charm on a leather cord rested between her breasts.

"I'll do my best," she said finally, perhaps realizing he'd been struck dumb by the sight of her. "But I can hardly comply with your demands when I don't know what they are."

Jack unglued his gaze from her body, lifting his focus to her face. A wicked gleam lit her eyes.

"You can start by letting me undress the rest." He stepped closer, forcing himself to keep his touch light. Functional. If he got caught up in the feel of her now, he might not be able to pry his hands away long enough to play this game out. "I didn't get to see you naked in the hot tub last night and it's an image that's been wreaking havoc with my head all day."

Unfastening her shorts, he let them fall to the deck around her bare feet. Her hips were clad in the same pink cotton as her breasts, the fabric soft as a T-shirt, yet still not as soft as what was inside. He tucked a finger under the waistband of her panties and flicked them lower over her hips. When they slid off to join her shorts, he turned his attention to her bra, working hooks free until she stood naked and unbelievable in front of him. True to her word, she'd let him undress her without helping, keeping her hands to herself.

"You're doing well," he whispered, gathering her up in his arms and positioning her over the hot tub. "You can get in while I enjoy the view."

Lowering her onto the small sun shelf built into the hot tub, Jack slid Alicia into the water while he remained on deck. Just like the previous night. Only now there were no clothes in the way when he looked at her. The jets churned the water and hid parts of her in a white froth, but her breasts bobbed enticingly at the surface, the nipples dark pink and slick.

Perfect for tasting.

"Well, I have to admit, this is a pretty easy gig so

far." Alicia lifted her arms to redo the knot in her hair, magically keeping most of it out of the water.

"I just wanted to take my time and go slow with you." Pulling off his shirt, he put his feet into the water near her and leaned close enough to massage her shoulders from behind. "Sometimes we wind each other up so much, so fast, that I don't get to savor all the details. I figured if I could make you be still—"

"You'd get to dictate the pace." She arched her neck when he touched her, rubbing her temple against the inside of his forearm as he moved from her shoulders down the front of her to explore the swell of her cleavage. "You get to drive me crazy while I have no chance to return the favor."

She gasped as he reached the tight peaks of her breasts and thumbed the tips. He cupped the hot, rushing water around her curves, watching the way the bubbles clung to her skin and slid down the sloping mounds.

"Not true," he assured her. "Just looking at you tests my restraint."

In fact, he needed to be in the tub with her sooner rather than later.

"Yeah?" She appeared genuinely surprised for a moment before he rose to undress.

Maybe the lightning-fast speed with which he peeled off his clothes helped convince her how close he was to the brink. Certainly the erection he sported had to communicate a whole hell of a lot about how much he needed her. He found a condom in his discarded clothes and set it near the edge of the tub.

By now, the sun had set fully, leaving them in darkness except for the light inside the tub. Jack slid into the bubbling beside her, the narrow size intended for two. There were seats built into it, but he wasn't there to relax. He wrapped his arms around Alicia and pulled her against him. She was hot and slick everywhere. His hands glided easily over her shoulders and down her arms.

To her waist and belly. Her hips. She tried to circle her arms around his neck, but he pinned her wrists to her sides and steered her closer to a wall of jets in the tub.

She squealed as the stream of water surged against her skin. He aligned one nozzle toward her right breast and another toward her left, holding her steady in the onslaught. Then, skimming his palms down her waist to her hips, he steered her so the cradle of her thighs landed in front of yet another jet. Jack could tell when he got the stream just right because her whole body bucked and rocked against him, the orgasm shuddering through her almost on contact.

"Jack!" Eyes closed, she leaned back into him, the soft curves of her bottom nudging his shaft. Reminding him how much more he needed from her.

But he savored the moment first. Her cheeks were flushed bright pink even in the dull glow of blue light from the tub. Water droplets congregated on her dark, spiky lashes. Her hair floated around her in the small pool, the blond waves encircling him like a mermaid's locks.

"This is what I wanted to see," he whispered in her ear when the shudders had eased. "You. Just like this."

Slowly, her eyelids lifted, her dark eyes locking with his as she peered back at him over her shoulder.

"It was…more rewarding than I expected, to be compliant." She licked her lips with a slow sweep of her tongue. "I think I could be convinced to do it again sometime."

"I'm holding you to that." He spun her in his arms, unable to wait any longer for what he wanted.

"I want you to hold me to *this*." She wriggled against the hard length of his cock, driving him out of his mind in two seconds flat.

Apparently she'd already punched the clock on submissive. She was like a firecracker that didn't stop once she got started—all motion and heat. Her hands traced wet paths down his chest before disappearing under the water.

To surround him.

The sensation drained all thoughts of who was in charge. There was only Alicia and the feel of her everywhere, all over him. Her mouth on his. Her teeth nipping his lower lip before trailing slick kisses down the column of his throat.

She palmed the condom and put it in his hand, the salt water in the tub not affecting it since it was still in the package. Vaguely, he realized they ought to at least lie on the sun shelf in more shallow water—where they wouldn't be immersed—so the condom would still work.

Hooking his arms under hers, he lifted Alicia up and set her where he wanted her, water sluicing off her body as their skin steamed in the cooler air. Being careful to keep her at least partially submerged so she would stay warm, he unwrapped the prophylactic and rolled it on.

He nudged her thighs apart and entered her. A low, throaty moan hummed like music in his ear as she arched her hips up, giving him better access. Taking the full length of him.

She looked so beautiful. So delicate and pale in the blue light as her hair swirled in the water beneath her. Her eyes locked with his, assuring him that she was right there with him in every way possible. Present to the moment. All his.

Possessiveness surged through him in a primal rush. He wanted her on a fundamental level. Thrusting hard, he pinned her hips down, holding her steady to imprint the moment on her as thoroughly as it would forever be imprinted on him.

When his release came, it pulsed hot and hard, his body straining inside her, reaching deep. Alicia's soft feminine muscles milked every last spasm from him, contracting around him like a tight fist, until they lay spent in the shallow water.

At some point, they'd need to have dinner. Make conversation again.

But for now, he wished they could stay here forever. Unaffected by old mistakes. Taking pleasure from each other. Not worrying about the separation that awaited them at the end of this journey if Alicia didn't give him a second chance.

8

"WHILE LOSING THE BET was admittedly fun, I still say you cheated." Alicia speared a bite of her dinner as they sat at the table near the helm.

They were farther out to sea now, but Jack had headed for a string of tiny islands to set the anchor for a couple hours so they could eat without worrying about navigating in the dark. There were no marinas or even developments on the smattering of rocky outcroppings nearby, but the water was shallow enough for the long-line anchor to hit bottom. He'd killed the engine and left the lights on for other boats to see. Not that there was traffic out here at this time of night. They hadn't seen a boat since long before sunset.

Now, he savored a forkful of the silver hake she'd cooked for his dinner. Victory tasted sweet. Especially with the memories of everything else they'd shared tonight.

"A bet's a bet," he reminded her, adjusting the height of the flame on the hurricane lamp between them. "And you have to admit my fish dwarfed yours by a couple hundred pounds."

"But you didn't technically catch it if you didn't drag it on board," she grumbled, lifting her wineglass to her lips.

Even in the candlelight he could see the high color in her cheeks from the day in the sun. A sun-bleached-blonde strand blew against her jaw and skimmed along her throat. She wore a lemon-yellow hoodie over the layered tank tops she'd sported most of the day. No makeup and no jewelry were in sight; Alicia required no decoration. There was a strength and competence about her that drew his eyes like no other woman he'd ever met.

"Did you really want me to haul in what was probably a northern bluefin tuna—a species that is seriously overfished?" He cut more bread from a baguette she'd warmed in the galley oven with some herbs and olive oil. "Because if I went to the trouble of pulling an *Old Man and the Sea* we would have had to sit at this table until we choked down all three hundred pounds of that sucker."

He didn't believe in catching fish you weren't going to eat. And since Keith's cushy corporate toy didn't come equipped with a fish locker, that meant they could catch only what would fit in the galley's refrigerator.

"I *am* hungry, but maybe not that hungry," she finally conceded, a hint of a smile curving her lips. "Plus the cleaning would have taken forever."

"Dinner is fantastic, by the way." He lifted his glass

in a toast, the white wine catching the candlelight and casting watery reflections on the table. "Cheers to the chef."

"Thank you." She clinked her glass to his. "We lucked out that Keith keeps the pantry nicely stocked."

"Along with the wine fridge." Jack had found a temperature-controlled drawer in the galley that held ten bottles ranging from pinot grigio to Chianti. "So how often do you talk to Keith? I didn't know you kept in touch with the family."

"I didn't for a long time. But Keith remembered my water sports business a couple years ago, and asked me to take some clients out for a day of kite-boarding lessons. It was a big job for me and it went so well that he recommended me to some other bigwig types who did the same thing. Those group sessions really boosted my income and grew my reputation in a hurry."

Jack would have to thank his brother for helping her out like that. He studied her in the candlelight for a long moment while the waves lapped the side of the boat, rocking them gently. The rhythm was slow and easy, kind of like the way he wanted to take her again tonight. He didn't want to take one moment for granted.

"What are you going to do with all your loyal customers when you move to Bar Harbor?" He guessed she must have built quite a following if that was her only business and it had generated enough profit for the down payment on a bed-and-breakfast.

"They'll get a discount coupon for a weekend at my

new inn and a free lesson with me once I reestablish a water sports business up there."

He nodded, seeing the benefit of that. No doubt she'd fill the rooms on her new property for at least a few nights with that deal. It would be a hell of a lot easier to be happy for her if she were planning all this for an inn on the Cape. He'd help her fill those rooms, damn it. In fact, he'd be sure he kept one on standby for all the nights he wanted to be with her.

"You don't miss the event planning you used to do with my dad?" How could she walk away from everything—everyone—she knew? "I seem to recall you were having a great time at the charity golf event where I first asked you out."

"Not really. I like to entertain people on a smaller scale than that. I was just having so much fun that night because you couldn't take your eyes off me." She pushed her plate aside and folded her arms on the table, fixing him with her dark gaze.

His heart thudded hard in his chest.

"I remember." He'd fought the attraction for months. But that night, it had seemed as if she was everywhere and he couldn't escape how much he wanted her. "You laughed during the follow-through of my drive and my shot sliced into the woods so far I thought I'd never find the ball."

He'd been off his game, to say the least. She'd filled up every corner of his mind, not leaving room for anything else.

"You must have had bionic hearing," she protested—

the argument was almost as old as their acquaintance. "I was on the eighth hole and you were on the ninth."

"What can I say? Your laugh can turn me on from a mile away." He'd hardly been able to finish his game, torn between a desire to stay below par and the need to drop his clubs and hunt down Alicia.

"Then how come you needed the bet with Ryan before you even walked over to me that night?" She swirled her wine in her glass and avoided his gaze.

He'd confessed long ago that his older brother had egged him on, betting he would never get a kiss from their dad's sexy young intern. Jack hadn't been able to let the jab slide, countering that he'd have a kiss in less than five minutes.

Alicia had never seemed to mind being the subject of a wager. But now, he wondered if he'd misunderstood her easy acceptance of that gamble. Her concentration on the wine in her stemware made him think his answer mattered more to her than she'd care to admit.

"I knew it wasn't a good time to get involved with someone—I was flying to Rome on business a week later."

"There's never been a good time for us, has there?" She set aside her unfinished wine. "First I was too young. Then you didn't want me to wait for you while you were in the navy."

He couldn't read her mood. But he sensed an undercurrent of tension—her frustration with him.

"*Now* is a good time." He'd turn this boat around and make serious time back to the Cape if she would agree. He'd be home twice as fast as they'd gotten this far, thanks to the prevailing winds.

"Only because of another bet, right?" She pushed his plate to the side so there was a clear path between them to lean farther across the small table. Her fingers brushed his chest. Right over the steady thump of his heart. "I ended up with you tonight because of a contest for sexual favors."

And didn't that sound sordid as hell all of a sudden? He hadn't meant it that way.

"We're not together because of any bet." He clamped his hand around her wandering fingers, unwilling to take things further if she had any reservations about his motives. No matter how much he wanted her. "It's a good time for us now because we're older and wiser, plus there's still one hell of a spark between us. Come back home with me and we can explore this thing without a time limit. Without the impending deadline of Bar Harbor hanging over us."

She stilled in his grip.

"I seem to recall you weren't terribly concerned about imposing deadlines on our relationship when you were the one who wanted to stretch his wings." She didn't spell it out, but she was clearly trying to equate his commitment to the navy with her desire to run a bed-and-breakfast in Maine.

Another time, he might have debated the point with her, but right now, he realized he had zero desire to do battle. He didn't want to waste a second of what little time they might have left together. They'd be in Bar

Harbor tomorrow no matter how much he dragged his feet on the rest of the voyage.

"You're right," he conceded. Picking up his napkin, he waved it. "See my white flag? I surrender."

"That fast?" She blinked and peered over her shoulder. "Where did my competitive ex-boyfriend disappear to?"

Jack wasn't so sure himself, but his best guess was that he wasn't the same man she'd dated four years ago. Since returning home, he hadn't made a plan for what he would do when he saw her, but he'd always imagined he'd at least look her up. He'd hoped she was single, knowing neither of her relationships after him had lasted very long.

Seeing her here on Keith's boat—holding her in his arms and remembering what they'd been like together— had forced Jack's hand where she was concerned. If he didn't make a play for her now, he'd never be with her again. And the thought of her stepping off this boat without looking back made his chest ache with a hollowness he couldn't deny.

"You know we'll arrive in Maine by tomorrow afternoon, right?" He loosened his hold on her hands, trailing his thumb over her knuckles and down each finger.

Her skin was smooth. Perfect.

"I guessed we'd get there pretty quickly once we moved away from the coastline." She glanced down at their hands.

"Since there is an undeniable deadline involved with our arrival, I don't want to waste one second between then and now arguing about anything. Not who caught the bigger fish or who owes who a sexual favor. I want a truce for as long as we're on this boat together."

Mostly, he wanted *her*—every second between now and when they docked.

AS FAR AS ALICIA WAS concerned, it was a perfect metaphor for their relationship that they were adrift at sea in the dark. Actually, the comparison could only be more apt if she jumped overboard again. Any way she looked at the situation, she was in too deep with Jack. She didn't know where they were headed, but she couldn't let go of him if she tried.

Tomorrow, in Bar Harbor, she would sort it all out.

Tonight, the only lighthouse on the horizon was what she felt for Jack.

"A truce." She nodded, the movement jerky thanks to the buzz of anticipation that vibrated through her limbs. "I like that. But I don't think that means we need to forgo sexual favors."

Her voice didn't resemble her own in her ears, the low, throaty murmur seeming to belong to someone else.

"No?" His shoulder muscles bunched as he leaned across the table, impossibly close. His lips brushed hers lightly. "Maybe we could make an exception as long as the recipient is willing to give as good as he gets."

His tongue teased a path along her lower lip, sending a pleasurable shiver down her spine. Her world narrowed to the stubble-rough feel of his jaw against her face. The scents of ocean and aftershave.

"I trust you implicitly on that one." She lifted a hand to his cheek and traced the outline of the dramatic bone structure that helped give all the Murphy men their good looks. "You're very generous that way."

He broke the kiss to rise, tug her out of her seat and into his arms.

They stood, feet braced on the gently swaying boat, sizing each other up in the glow of the hurricane lamp and the white light that shone from the boat's highest point. Her heart raced with the desire to wrap herself around the sexy stud in front of her. She was playing with fire, being with him, but was irresistibly drawn to his dark good looks and the wicked gleam in his green eyes. Jack was a man of endless capabilities, a man she respected.

A man who could scald her skin with one sizzling touch.

Swallowing hard, she unzipped her hoodie and slid it off. Mostly, she wanted to peel off layers to feel even closer to Jack when she touched him. But seeing the way his eyes widened at the sight of her in a couple of thin, layered tank tops, she was even more gratified with her decision to start undressing.

"Like what you see, Murphy?" She couldn't help asking the question. Her heart had ached over him long enough that she would gladly rake in all the affirmation—verbal and otherwise—that he wanted her now.

"I'll tell you when I see a little more." He tucked two

fingers beneath the straps on her shoulder and nudged them off.

The heat of his gaze stroked the tops of her breasts as surely as a caress, causing the tips to pebble. Her breath hitching, she reached for the drawstring on the lounge pants she'd worn around the galley for cooking, letting the bright, printed flannel fall into a heap at her feet. As the night breeze hit her bare thighs and wound around her cotton bikini panties, she flattened a palm to his chest.

Beneath the gray T-shirt he wore, his skin radiated heat like a furnace. The flames practically danced up her fingers as she touched him.

"I like what I see," he finally admitted. "A whole lot." He returned his touch to her other shoulder, pulling the straps down on that side. "So much that I can't wait to see everything. Feel everything. Taste everything."

He wrapped his hands around her waist and drew her to him until she fit snug against him, then he dropped a kiss to her bare shoulder and peeled her shirts down, exposing her breasts to his questing mouth.

Nerve endings fired to life all over. Alicia's head lolled back as she gave up command of her body to his touch. His tongue.

He licked at the taut peak of one nipple, sending her into a paroxysm of sensual shivers. A hungry moan ripped from her throat and she threaded her fingers through his hair, holding him there as he feasted on one breast and then the other.

Sweet warmth curled in her belly, melting the place

between her thighs. Unsure how to communicate the new ache requiring his attention, she rolled her hips against the rock-hard length behind the fly of his cargo shorts. His thigh was between her legs in an instant, pressing right where she needed. Right where she wanted.

But that relief was fleeting, too, driving a deeper hunger.

"Maybe I should be the one to offer up sexual favors now." His voice rumbled in her ear.

"Okay." She nodded helplessly, trembling so badly her fingers shook and her temples tingled. She was all sensation and reaction. "Although it seems I like to give them as much as receive them."

Her last favor had taught her plenty about what he liked, and she couldn't wait to deploy that particular sensual weapon again. But now, waiting to see what he had in mind, she wanted nothing more than to have him inside her. He surprised her by picking her up and carrying her down the steps into the cabin below.

"You're dragging me back to your cave," she mused as her eyes adjusted to the dark, wondering what he had in mind. "I thought men were visual creatures who like to see what's happening."

"I do." He switched on a night-light near the door that glowed red, a color that would help a sailor maintain his night vision if he had to go back on deck. "But I can see well enough now."

Depositing her in the middle of the dark blue bedspread, he stood over her. He remained fully dressed, while she'd kept on only a pair of panties and a tank top that drifted down around her waist.

"I can't give you much of a striptease, if that's what you're looking for." She skimmed a hand along her bare breasts. "I'm mostly naked, anyhow. But I can think of another favor you might like...."

She reached out to palm the bulge in his shorts. To stroke him.

His eyelids drifted closed for an instant before he appeared to force them back open.

"No." He gripped her wrist, imprisoning her gently. "The favor I want requires you to shut your eyes."

Feeling highly compliant with whatever he requested, she did as he asked, plunging herself into darkness while he hovered over her at the foot of the bed.

Cool night air blew in through the cabin window, whispering over her fevered skin while he made shuffling sounds that suggested he was removing his clothes. She debated taking a peek, but before she acted on the impulse, he knelt between her thighs.

Her eyes flew open as his fingers curved around her hips, holding her still.

"That's *my* favor to *you?*" She couldn't deny a surge of arousal at the sight of his broad, tanned hands on her skin, his shoulder sliding beneath her thigh.

Slowly, deliberately, he rubbed his jaw along the soft cotton of her panties, just above the place that throbbed for his touch.

"Maybe it's a favor for both of us. But what I need from you right now is for you to lie still and let me do whatever I please." He nipped at her hip with his teeth, then clamped down on the lace hem of her underwear, drawing the bikini bottoms down.

Down.

Lying still wouldn't have been an option as he worked the fabric lower, except that he held her tight, pinning her hips to the mattress. Her toes curled and her fingers twisted in the bedspread. His touch and his presence between her thighs would have been devastating enough all on their own.

But the memory of his words smoked through her consciousness, calling to mind the last time he'd said them to her. That was the night he'd taken her virginity, which she'd been coming out of her skin to give to him....

"WHAT I WANT IS FOR YOU to lie still and let me do whatever I please." Jack's tone brooked no argument.

Another woman might have been put out by the caveman tactics in bed, but Alicia loved it. Loved him. She fought with him and competed with him in every other facet of their relationship, but didn't mind giving up her power in the bedroom. The thought of him doing whatever he pleased to her sent the early-warning tremors of an orgasm rippling through her.

He'd taken her out on his new sailboat to christen it. He'd called it the Vesta *after her, since she joked about being a Vestal virgin. Being a twenty-year-old virgin hadn't bothered her before meeting Jack, since she'd never been in a relationship that seemed worthy of getting physical. But Jack Murphy was more than a hot guy. He was smart. Principled. Funny. Completely unintimidated by her swimming prowess and her strength. In fact, Jack encouraged her to be as competitive and opinionated as she pleased.*

Except for right now, when he was finally going to initiate her into the mysteries of womanhood.

"I'm dying," she said, twisting beneath him as he stroked the slick center of her. "I'm so ready for this."

She could feel his grin against her stomach when he kissed her navel.

"Who did we decide was in charge?" The hot whisper along her skin made her whimper in frustration.

They'd stripped off their clothes at least ten minutes ago, after they had anchored near an uninhabited island off the coast of Chatham. The secluded cove offered plenty of privacy, allowing them to roll around on a blanket on deck, under the stars.

"I just don't want to miss this orgasm that's so close if you would—"

Stretching up to cover her body, he silenced her with a kiss. She couldn't think when he kissed her. No doubt that's why he did it. His hand covered her sex, one finger stirring the molten core....

She flew apart instantly, seeing far more stars behind her eyes than they'd spotted over the sea that night.

"There's more where that came from," he promised, his words breaking through the sensual haze that held her spellbound. "But you have to behave...."

"JACK." Alicia's hips stirred against his grip as she strained to get closer to him. "Please."

He eased back enough to remove her panties before he took his place between her thighs again.

"So impatient." He stroked a finger down the center of her sex. "So beautiful."

She couldn't find her voice to say anything either way. Her whole body tensed, every fiber of her being keenly attuned to his touch. His warmth. His powerful shoulders under her thighs, holding her steady for the slow circling of his thumb.

Her breath came fast, and her breasts were tight and aching, as if they'd never get enough of him. When his tongue replaced his thumb between her legs, the pleasure was so exquisite she had to fight off the release that threatened then and there. Desire flooded her veins in a dark, delicious tide. She twisted against the mattress and managed to hang on a little longer, to savor the feel of delectable tension inside her.

She wanted him everywhere at once. The velvet stroke of his mouth on her made her mindless. She gripped his shoulders, his body the only steady thing in a world threatening to splinter apart at any moment.

When release came, the waves of sensation convulsed through her. He held her tighter, closer, urging her on until every last shattering tremor had quieted. Only then did he relinquish his grip on her hips, placing one last kiss on her sex before he arched over her.

Dazed and hungry for him, she blinked up into his eyes. He studied her in the red glow from the night-light as he tugged open the nightstand drawer and retrieved the condom stash. Two left. One of which he'd already freed to sheathe himself.

She levered up on an elbow to kiss him, tasting her own desire on his tongue. He positioned himself between her legs, never breaking the kiss.

He entered her in a thrust that brought one final aftershock pulsing through her muscles, which clenched him tight. Glancing up, she found his green eyes on her, watching her with a heated intensity that threatened to burn deep into her heart.

The look—the moment—hit her hard. Closing her eyes, she fought to untangle the past from the present, to steal only pleasure from their joining.

"Ally." He broke the kiss to breathe her name over her lips and wrap her in his arms.

With his chest pressed to hers, his hard, muscular thighs stretched beside her legs, he was suddenly everywhere at once, just like she'd wanted. He cupped her cheek with one hand, her hip with the other, and initiated a deep, slow rhythm as he moved inside her. Each thrust took her higher. Every withdrawal left her gasping for more.

She speared her fingers through his dark hair, anchoring herself to him as he moved. He answered by cupping her breast and tweaking the taut nipple between his thumb and forefinger. Her heartbeat sped as she climbed toward the peak of pleasure all over again. Faster, higher.

Deeper.

"Ally," he whispered again, calling her to be present in the moment with him.

She understood what he wanted, and she couldn't resist the invitation any more than she'd been able to hold back from him four years ago. Or yesterday.

Opening her eyes, she sank into his gaze as surely as if she'd dived headfirst. He was all around her. Inside her.

In her heart.

And as the first gorgeous wave of fulfillment broke over her, Alicia had to acknowledge that he'd never really left.

9

"WHAT TIME IS YOUR meeting with the property owner?" Jack asked when he spotted Alicia glancing at her watch for the third time the next day.

They'd taken shifts at the helm starting shortly before dawn, making steady headway toward Bar Harbor. He would rather have stayed anchored there, enjoying every second of being with Alicia. But just like the previous day, she'd pulled away in the aftermath of what they'd shared during the long, heated night. Yesterday, she'd spent time sketching the bed-and-breakfast, losing herself in the silence of drawing. Today, she moved around the boat in a flurry of activity, cleaning the galley, packing her bag, folding and storing the curtain he'd put up to keep the rain off the helm in the storm.

Obviously, she was dead set on not getting any more involved than their blow-your-mind sex required. The realization forced him to see that he would need to take more drastic measures if he wanted a second chance with her. Alicia had no intention of returning to Chatham—or him—if she could help it.

Maybe he'd underestimated how much his detour into the navy had hurt her. Maybe her leaving his ass today would be well-deserved payback.

He'd be haunted by memories of this time together for the rest of his days. No other woman would ever bring him to the kind of mind-blowing precipice she could.

"One o'clock." She tapped her watch with a fingernail as he steered closer to the coastline. "My appointment was originally for four this afternoon, but I asked if I could move it up once I knew we'd arrive early."

"Can't wait to get rid of me?" Jack rechecked his heading to be sure they were still on course, the engine humming steadily as they cut through the gentle waves.

Along the coast, stands of pines were interspersed with houses and rocky outcroppings. Even in its most developed spots, Maine bore little resemblance to the crowded tumble of mansions and cottages that stood side by side on most of Cape Cod. The cooler weather and rougher waters welcomed a hardier tourist. Sapphire-blue waves sparkled in the sunlight, crashing in frothy spray on jagged rocks along the shore. The day had dawned clear and bright, too damn cheery for saying goodbye to a woman he'd only just welcomed back into his life.

"No." She grinned at him over her shoulder. Hair tied in a low ponytail, she wore a burgundy sweatshirt with Boston College on the front. In khaki shorts despite the cooler weather, she looked every inch the college coed he'd fallen for the first time around. "But I'm really eager to spend as much time as I can scouting the property before it gets dark. I'm glad I'll have a few more hours to check things out."

Her words reminded him she was far from a college coed. She was a woman who'd saved enough to purchase her dream property far away from him. No matter that she had opportunities back at home; Alicia was striking out on her own to create a special retreat that would be a unique reflection of her. He'd seen as much in the notes she'd made.

His chest ached to realize how little time he had left.

"Alicia…" He searched for words, unsure what he wanted to ask. He didn't really have the right to ask anything.

"There it is!" Her voice lifted an octave or two. She pointed toward the shore with one hand. "It's beautiful!"

Cutting the power on the engine, Jack slowed the boat and moved toward the rail on the foredeck beside her. He followed her gaze to the rambling three-story structure that had probably been some wealthy family's summer cottage at one time. A turn-of-the-century home built on two levels, it was about the same size as Jack's parents' home back in Chatham, which was ten thousand square feet. The resemblance ended there, however. Because the bed-and-breakfast property, while a definite diamond in the rough, needed a great deal of work. Overgrown gardens obscured porches that appeared slightly crooked. The yellow clapboard siding needed power washing and possible replacing, the edges dark with wear or rot.

He was about to say she had her work cut out for her when she clutched his arm with both hands.

"I'm so excited." She stared up at him with a warm glow in her dark brown eyes. Her cheeks were flushed pink like a kid's at Christmas. "Thank you for bringing me up here."

He couldn't help but remember the last time he'd seen high color in her cheeks. It hadn't been that many hours ago and she'd been underneath him, lavishing a litany of praise on the talent of his hands. With an effort, he blinked away the memory.

"You're welcome." He didn't know what else to say. Telling her she was crazy to invest in something that couldn't be profitable without some serious restoration would hardly be appreciated.

"I know you're seeing all the flaws right now." Relinquishing his arm, she gripped the rail and studied the looming property perched on a prime piece of real estate that nudged out into the water so that the house would have ocean views on three sides. "But I've crunched a lot of numbers on what I can afford and it's *going* to *work*."

Something about the way she emphasized the words made him wonder if she'd based part of those calculations on the fact that she was incredibly stubborn and persistent. Those qualities had made her a champion swimmer and a successful apprentice in his father's company. But no amount of personal grit would make up for the fact that she needed to pour in a lot of capital to get her dream off the ground.

How would she manage all this on her own?

"Hey, you don't have to convince me. You could tackle Everest if you set your mind to it." He cupped her shoulder and squeezed it, hoping she knew that he believed in her. "I know you'll make it work if you want it to."

"Thank you." She tipped her chin to smooth her cheek over his fingers where he touched her, rubbing against him like a cat. "That means a lot to me."

Surprised at the warmth in her voice, he was grateful he'd chosen that approach instead of listing all the potential pitfalls of the place. Still, he didn't want to see her get in over her head when he could help her make a better decision.

"You know, I don't have a strict time frame for dropping off the boat to Keith's colleague. I'd love to walk around the property with you if you don't mind the company."

The original plan had been to drop her off at the inn while he cruised farther north to deliver the boat to Keith's colleague.

"Yeah?" She lifted an eyebrow as if to size up the offer. "I guess that would be okay as long as you don't try to burst my bubble."

"I'll make you a deal."

"Our bets have a way of working out well for me even when I lose."

The fishing contest had been a pleasure for them both.

"This one isn't a bet, exactly. Can we agree that I'll give my honest input on everything I see—just as I would with one of my brothers? But only if you want to hear it. It'll be up to you."

"Deal." She held out her hand to shake on it.

He checked the horizon as they drifted inland. The engine was off. They were still in deep water.

With that all-clear, he ignored her hand and pulled her against him.

"I've got a better way to seal the bargain." He tipped her chin up for a better angle, giving her time to back away if she wanted.

She didn't. She stared up into his eyes, waiting.

Some of the fear that had gripped his chest earlier eased. Alicia wasn't giving him the boot. At least not yet. He'd bought himself a few hours. And who knew? Maybe he could talk her into one more night.

In the interest of hedging his bets, he kissed her as if she was the only woman in the world. Because for him, he realized, she really was.

ALICIA GRIPPED Jack's shoulders, the hot, hard wedges of muscle contracting at her touch.

She came to life every time he put his hands on her; it was as simple as that. Her days without Jack had been bland—a black-and-white landscape compared to the vivid, high-definition world her life became when he walked through it. Her senses were on high alert, aware of every nuance around her. The scent of Jack's soap mingled with the sea air in a fragrance she would always associate with him alone. The feel of his heart beating was like a metronome that set the pace for a whole symphony of exquisite responses within her. Pleasure wound through her, thick and slow, as she slid her tongue along his in a dance she could never tire of.

Time stood still on the deck of the boat. The wind blew by them; the water lapped at the hull. Gulls screeched overhead and the sounds of life on the shore began to drift closer, but none of it mattered when she was in Jack's arms.

He could fill her world if she let him. Reduce it to moments spent with him. He was that powerful of a presence and she was that susceptible to his spell.

"Jack." She forced herself back a step, dragging in breaths of clean sea air to cool the fever within.

Her body tingled in the wake of the kiss, every atom demanding she return to where she had been just a moment ago—pressed against Jack.

"Mmm?" He lazily drew a thumb over her damp lower lip, his gaze lingering on her mouth, as though contemplating another taste.

In that moment, she had her first inkling of how hard it was going to be to say goodbye when he left Bar Harbor. It made her want to kiss him every second until then, to fill up her memory stores for a future without him.

If relationships could be based solely on kissing, she

would have found a match made in heaven. Too bad they were at odds on so many other things.

"We'd better get to shore," she said, unable to come up with any solid reason for why she wanted to end the kiss. She didn't dare confide her fear that she'd lose her heart to him for a second time if she kissed him without a certain amount of discipline. "I don't meet the owner for a little longer, but he said if I was early I could walk the grounds."

"We can do that," Jack agreed, his gaze moving toward shore. "But how about if—while I steer the boat in, you explain to me all the things this property has that you can't get anywhere on Cape Cod."

Thankfully, his words reminded her why she shouldn't allow herself to be swept away by his kiss. He didn't like the idea of her moving to Bar Harbor, and would resist it for reasons she couldn't fully understand. Edging out of his grip, she gave a short nod.

"Fine. But if I do that, you have to tell me why it's so important to you that I don't leave the Cape."

"One—the Cape has more tourists." Jack moved to the helm to engage the state-of-the-art steering system, which featured a joystick. The improved maneuverability made docking a quick and precise process. "Two—you will be happier and therefore more personally successful if you can stay closer to your family and friends."

As Alicia listened to his list, she realized that he'd told her most of these things already. Maybe she hadn't wanted to believe his motives were purely unselfish because a part of her still wished he wanted her back. Perhaps she'd hoped he would tell her that he wanted to be close to her.

But as he hit reason number six—something involving her potential profit margin—she realized such a confession was not forthcoming. It had been foolish of her to even dream of it.

"Okay. You made your point." She helped him tie up the boat now that he had the craft right where he wanted it.

A long wooden pier extended into the water from the inn's property. Only one other boat was tied up there, but Jack still took the precaution of keeping Keith's vessel on the opposite side of the planked dock.

"I only want what's best for you," he reiterated, confirming how fanciful she'd been to think he wanted anything else from her.

"Well, I want a fresh start and I can't get that in Cape Cod." She decided that listing her reasons for this move was a good idea right about now. Faced with Jack's undiluted appeal, she needed to erect some defenses in a hurry.

"A fresh start," he repeated as he tied a knot around one of the cleats on the dock. "You make it sound as if you can't wait to get away from Chatham, and I'm not sure why. You always liked it there before." He frowned, pausing in his work with the knot. "Did something bad happen there that I don't know about?"

If the storm cloud on his brow was any indication, Jack Murphy was fully prepared to go medieval on anything or anyone that gave her trouble. The notion made her smile.

"No." Except for Jack breaking up with her. And technically, that had happened in Boston, while she was at school.

"You're not trying to teach your dad a lesson for ignoring his only daughter?" Jack stepped up onto the dock and then held his hand out to Alicia to help her do the same. "Because I know he's checked out on you plenty of times. And that—payback for being an absentee father—I can understand."

She took his hand as she hoisted herself onto the pier. Such a simple touch. Such an immediate, electric reaction.

Quickly, she withdrew her fingers and stuffed them in the pocket of her hoodie.

"Nothing like that." She shook her head and then wondered if it had been a mistake not to simply take the easy out he'd offered her. She couldn't very well admit she didn't want to be a witness to his dating life now that he was back home from the navy. "I'm just not sure I'll be taken seriously in Chatham. You know, the prophet can't preach in his hometown? That kind of thing. Whereas if I move far away, no one will have preconceived ideas about me. I think it'll be easier to get the business up and running."

He frowned, his steps slowing as they reached the end of the pier. "I don't buy it."

"Excuse me?" How could he have guessed her real reasons for wanting to get the heck out of Dodge?

"Most small businesses have more success when their owner is entrenched in the community. Plus, you're both well-known and well-liked."

"But remember, I don't want to compete with your father's resorts." She glanced around the property, which she already knew well from photos.

A tire swing hung from an old oak tree. Tall pines sheltered the main building from prevailing winds. A shed they called a boathouse served as a repository for their limited supply of water gear—a couple canoes and life jackets. Worn Adirondack chairs nestled under the porch eaves. Stone-covered paths connected the various facets of the property, from a rock garden to a fire pit, over to a picnic table near the small patch of beach.

"The clientele you'd draw with a bed-and-breakfast is entirely different from the guests who seek out a resort. That's not even a factor," Jack continued, oblivious to the fact that she'd already started picking out colors to paint the Adirondack chairs.

"I should have one in every color," she murmured, moving toward a broken lounger near the fire pit.

"Ally?" he called, following her over the sloping expanse of scraggly lawn.

"Isn't it charming?" She ran a hand over the weatherworn back of the cedar chair.

"It's ready to fall apart." He pointed to the crack in the seat, apparently taking her comment literally.

"I mean the whole place." She waved to the rambling structure and the sunlit yard. "Can't you see it full of families on a summer weekend?"

She could already picture the collection of wooden boats she'd start for the little ones who wanted to play in the surf. Maybe she'd need a wading pool to give the youngest guests a safe place to paddle.

While she was waiting for his responses, she heard his cell phone chime. Jack pinched the bridge of his nose as he read a text message. Was he stressed by whatever note he'd received? Or because he couldn't talk her out of an idea he seemed oddly opposed to?

"I don't know why you hate this idea so much," she observed while he tucked his phone back into his pocket. She jogged a few steps to the tire swing, tipping it sideways to empty the rainwater filling the lower half. "You've had a chance to explore the world. I've been in Chatham saving my pennies so I could explore some, too. It'll be good for me to see new things. Have new experiences."

"I don't hate the idea." He followed her to the swing. "Want me to push you?"

"You don't need to ask twice." Grinning, she hopped onto the tire—legs through the center, hands on top. She balanced her chin on her hands while she waited for him to push her, admiring the view of the Atlantic. "I hope your message wasn't bad news."

She realized she hadn't asked him about his plans now that he was out of the service. Was he working on a business of his own?

"No. It was Kyle inviting us to one of his games tomorrow. Axel was traded to Kyle's team this season. It's the first year they've played together since college."

Kyle played hockey for the Boston Bears. She'd gone to see him once with a few friends from their graduating class, but it was after she and Jack had broken up, so she hadn't told Kyle she would be there. It had been fun but a little awkward, since her girlfriends had used the outing to quiz her about what had happened between her and Jack.

"In Boston?" She wouldn't be home that soon, as she wanted to spend a few days scoping out Bar Harbor.

"Montreal, actually. It's only a preseason game, but one of Axel's friends from college plays on the Canadian team so Axel and Kyle are jazzed about it." Jack hauled the swing backward like a carnival ride cranking up. "We should go."

He released her at the same moment he suggested they attend the game. The resulting *whoosh* in her belly was as much from Jack's surprise invitation as from flying through the air.

"We?" She turned to look at him to see if she had misunderstood. By then she was already winging her way back toward him, spinning and twirling as the tire twisted.

"Why not?" He shrugged as if a formal, planned date was no big deal. "I can snag us a private flight and we can grab some dinner before the game. You'll have to eat whether you're here or there. We can leave at five o'clock and be back by eleven."

Another hard push sent her sailing so high she kicked a tree branch with her tennis shoe.

She really had to tell him no. Her whole focus should

be buying the inn—a task she'd initiated in part to distance herself from him. So hopping on a plane and jetting off to Canada with him for the evening seemed really counterproductive.

On the other hand, hadn't she secretly envied him for all those globe-trotting trips he'd taken when she was stuck in college? When would she have the chance to do anything like this again if not with the Murphys? Luckily she had an enhanced driver's license from trips she'd taken on the swim team, so crossing the border wouldn't be a problem. And she knew Jack always carried his passport when he was on the water, just in case.

"Come on, Ally," Jack urged, his voice suddenly in her ear as he caught the swing and brought her to a halt, steadying her spinning world. "I dare you to take a risk. It'll be a blast and I'll have you back before midnight. What could possibly go wrong?"

She glanced up at him through her lashes, her heart still pounding from the unexpected ride and the thought of more alone time with Jack.

She could list all kinds of things that could go wrong, including ending up back in bed with him. Or worse, falling head over heels for a man who liked to call the shots.

But once her purchase of the inn went through, there'd be no going back to Chatham. If she wanted a few more memories of Jack to tuck away before they parted for good, she needed to stock up fast. And bottom line, she had as tough a time walking away from a dare as he did.

"I'll tell you what could go wrong, hotshot." She wriggled out of the tire swing and stood. Leaning closer, she poked a gentle finger into his rock-hard chest. "You could realize what a huge mistake you made when you broke up with me. But if you're willing to take the chance, I'll be your date just this once."

10

THERE WERE MORE PROBLEMS with Alicia's dream property than Jack could name.

Staring at a crack in the cellar wall the next afternoon, he debated how to tell her about all of them, since the owner, hungry for a sale, didn't seem to be forthcoming. Jack had stifled his gut instincts about the house the day before, after they'd taken the initial tour of the bed-and-breakfast. Trying to keep the peace and not "burst her bubble" as she put it, he had left her to take a room in the inn, while he slept on the boat. He'd hoped that after she'd had time to reflect on it, she would see the property's shortcomings.

Plus, on a personal level, he was doing his damnedest not to push his luck renewing their relationship. She'd agreed to the date tonight, a positive sign that had helped him keep his eye on the prize as he'd retreated to the catamaran by himself the night before. She'd been wound up and had wanted to call her father and brother to tell them about the turn-of-the-century money pit. Jack had given her some space, hoping she would miss him half as much as he was missing her.

And, of course, he'd figured her family would help talk her out of buying the bayside inn that had once belonged to a noted area sea captain. But this morning, when he'd met her for a late breakfast in the inn's restored kitchen, she'd been as upbeat and excited about the hospitality potential here as ever. The owner hadn't said squat about the roof, which needed new shingles and had already left water damage in four rooms. The crack in the cellar wall equaled even bigger problems. Since the owner wasn't cautioning her about the wooden structure's drawbacks, Jack would have to be the bad guy—at least until she called in a home inspector to really crawl through the place. Otherwise, she might invest a lot of time and hope in a property that just wasn't meant to be.

His phone chimed in his pocket and he dug it out, glad for a diversion from a thorny situation. Seeing his youngest brother's name on the caller ID, he answered appropriately.

"Hey, bro. Psyching yourself up for a hat trick tonight?" He turned away from the cellar wall and headed up the stairs to the outdoor entrance on one side of the building.

He hadn't been one bit surprised when Kyle had gotten called up to the NHL after his years as a college hockey star. The youngest Murphy had excelled in every sport he'd tried, setting school records in all of them. Eventually—after Axel had come to live with them—Kyle had decided to focus solely on hockey. And while the whole clan still talked smack to him on a regular basis to keep him humble, they were all proud as hell of his accomplishments.

"Actually, I took a puck to the face in our morning skate, so I'm not sure if I'll be in top form tonight. Just wanted to warn you so you didn't think I'd been out brawling last night."

Jack winced in empathy as he took a seat in one of the weather-worn Adirondack chairs overlooking the cove. "Ouch. Where'd you get hit?"

"Nose. But I think the break helped straighten it out from the last time I busted it."

"You mean the last time Danny busted it for you?" Jack had been on hand to witness one of the few times a brotherly wrestling match had drawn blood. "Will you do me a favor and keep that particular family anecdote under your hat tonight, man?"

The knock-down, drag-out had happened right before Daniel and Jack went into the navy. Kyle had warned Danny he was wearing his heart on his sleeve by trying to get himself deployed the second he heard camerawoman Stephanie Rosen had been kidnapped. The comment had led to an uncharacteristically hostile comeback, and before he knew it, Kyle's nose had taken a right turn. And stayed that way for the past four years.

"Afraid you'll scare Alicia off if she finds out we're barely tamed beneath the Brooks Brothers facade?"

Jack tipped his face into the afternoon sun. "I don't

think she's bought the facade for a long time. But I never fessed up to the whole mess with Christina and Stephanie being kidnapped, since we were keeping Mom's connection to the Marcels under wraps—"

Kyle whistled low on the other end of the phone. "What happened to all that older-brother wisdom you used to preach about being honest with the ladies?"

Something in Kyle's voice suggested he wasn't kidding anymore. He was calling Jack on the carpet for teaching his younger brothers one thing while practicing something else.

"You may find this hard to believe, but you don't always have all the answers at the ripe old age of twenty-five." Jack certainly regretted the decision. "Alicia confused me back then. I think I was looking for reasons to set her free. She was so young and I was—"

"Crazy about her. Yeah, I remember. I'll make it a brotherly duty to ensure she knows all your secrets so you can't hide anything from her in the future." In the background, Kyle spoke quietly to someone else before returning to the phone. A woman? Something about the soft exchange gave Jack that impression. "So are you going to lock that relationship down this time, or what?"

But his brain was still stuck on the idea that Kyle might be hiding the fact that he was dating someone.

"You dog," Jack accused simply, figuring he'd learn more from his brother's reaction than by asking him straight out. Besides, the Murphy way was to attack first, ask questions later.

"Don't know what you're talking about," Kyle lied

smoothly, his blasé tone confirming he was with a woman even as they spoke.

"You're seeing someone."

"Can I help it that I needed a nurse after I broke my nose? Axel has the bedside manner of a Rottweiler, so it's not like I can count on him." On Kyle's end of the phone, an answering feminine giggle sounded.

"You're busted." Jack turned as, behind him, the metal cellar door swung open and Alicia stepped outside. "But I'll wait to gather more evidence until I interrogate you tonight after your game," he said, tying up his call as he watched her trail her hand along a rickety rose arbor nearby.

Kyle firmed up who they needed to speak to at the call window for their passes into the locker room area after the game. Then, before they disconnected, he paused.

"Jack?"

"Yeah?" He rose from the chair, ready to finalize his plans with Alicia for the day.

Ready to discuss the problems with the property she adored.

"The whole family likes Alicia. You feel me? One mistake with her is enough."

Jack's eyes went to her and her sun-streaked blond waves. Her endless freckles and wide brown eyes.

But Jack saw more than her killer curves and full lips. He saw her drive and ambition. Her willingness to work hard for what she wanted in life.

"Agreed." He swallowed hard, knowing Kyle was right. "I'm going to try like hell to get it right this time."

Which meant he couldn't sidestep the awkward conversations. If he wanted Alicia back in his life for good, he'd have to tackle their disagreements head-on. He pocketed the phone and waited for inspiration on how to broach a topic that might well send her running.

"I didn't mean to eavesdrop," she began, edging past a terra-cotta pot of basil and oregano in a well-tended container garden. Apparently the inn owners spent more time on growing herbs than on keeping a roof over their heads. "But you were looking directly at me when you said you were trying to get something right...."

"That was Kyle," he explained. "My brother insisted that I be good to you." Jack closed the distance between them. "And I assured him I would do just that."

She cast a wary gaze up to the main house and then sidled into his arms, the scents of roses and ocean breeze clinging to her. "Yet you didn't sleep in my bed last night."

Heat rushed him like a full-on blitz. Being with her these last days had only increased his need for her. He would have thought that time together would take the edge off, but the hunger seemed to build by the hour.

"I was trying to—"

She pressed a finger briefly to his lips, gently halting his protest. "I know why you retreated. It was thoughtful of you, given how wound up I was last night. I stayed awake until after 2:00 a.m. reading articles online about restoration."

Frowning, he regretted that he hadn't already spoken to her about the shortcomings of the bed-and-breakfast.

"I didn't notice any lights on or I would have checked on you." He'd peered up at the seaside structure more than once, thinking about Alicia most of the night, anyhow. With an effort, he peeled himself away from her now, needing a clearer head for a discussion. "Do you have time to talk about the property now? I made a list of a few things you'll want to take into consideration."

With one hand, he brought out his cell phone, and with the other, he kept her close. Hitting a few buttons, he emailed the detailed write-up to her—one of the other reasons he'd returned to the boat last night. He hadn't trusted his ability to spell everything out in person, since they occasionally argued for the sake of arguing—or for the sake of making up. This was too important for him to get distracted in the middle of an explanation, so he'd put the salient points in black and white.

"It must be a long list," she remarked, glancing at the touch screen of his phone.

"I figured it would help me stay focused if I wrote it down. Sometimes we fire each other up when we talk."

There had been a time when Alicia would have taken that comment as an opening to flirt with him and show him how fast she could indeed fire him up. Yet now, her posture turned rigid, her lips tightening.

"Fair enough." She nodded. "But do you think we could save the list until after our date? I'd like to enjoy tonight without thinking about all the setbacks to my purchase of the inn."

Surprised, he studied her expression, searching for clues to her mood. Apparently she was as eager to delay the discussion of the bed-and-breakfast as he was.

"Are you sure?" He wondered if she'd regret going to the game with him when she read his assessment later.

"Very sure. I asked for your opinion on the property and I want to hear it. But for tonight, I'd like us to just enjoy each other. No business." She gazed up into his eyes with a mixture of hunger and wary hope.

And he couldn't deny he felt the same way.

They'd bought themselves a reprieve for a few hours. He had one evening to convince Alicia they belonged together.

IT WAS NO SURPRISE that traveling with Jack meant flying in style.

Alicia liked the quick check-through security at the small airport at the start of their journey. And the private plane he'd arranged came equipped with a full bar and all the amenities—not that she could indulge in anything more than seltzer water with her nerves strung tight about this first official "date" with Jack. He seemed as interested as she was in testing the waters of a relationship. Which was both fun and nerve-racking.

What if dating turned into another fiasco? Another broken heart?

She shut down her worries as they buckled their seat belts for takeoff in the sleek, small Cessna. The cabin was set up with four luxurious seats facing each other, conference style. Behind where she and Jack had settled, a deep sofa nestled into the back of the plane. Not exactly a bed, but an intriguing use of space nevertheless.

Sleeping alone in the old sea captain's home the night before, Alicia had realized how much she missed Jack. Longed for him.

Testing the leather seat now, she reclined all the way, while her seltzer water remained safely in the cup holder alongside her on a small table.

"This is awesome." She stretched out fully, right down to pointing her toes. "Will you look at the leg room?"

"If you don't behave, I'm going to tell the pilot that your seat isn't in the upright position." Jack pushed the button to lift the back of it.

"Anyone ever tell you that you're a wet blanket?" She shivered in anticipation as her electronic chair rose slowly to where he leaned over her.

The sight of him, scent of him—everything about him made her heart beat faster. And they were all alone. On their first real date in four years.

"My younger brothers. All the time." He shrugged as he released the button on her armrest, his shoulder brushing hers. "But I was a lot tougher on them than I am you."

She knew that a great deal of responsibility had fallen to Jack after the family moved from South Yarmouth out to the big house in Chatham. Robert Murphy's business interests had exploded in the early nineties, and his wife and eldest son had helped out as much as they could. That left Jack in charge of the younger boys. He'd said before that being a kid in charge of kids meant you had lots of responsibility and no real authority to back it up. No doubt that's where his need to take charge and protect others had started. Even when his autocratic ways bugged her, she had to admit he was good at it.

He didn't lay down the law to further his own agenda, the way her dad always had. Jack listened. He worked to come up with solutions that were fair for everyone. Except for when he left her…

Blinking back the old insecurity, she reached out to him, sliding an arm around his neck as the plane's engines grew louder. The growl of the motors rumbled through her, keeping pace with her racing heart. She wouldn't let the past rob her of the present with Jack.

"Has it ever occurred to you that it wouldn't hurt to play more and take charge less often?" Her fingers speared through the short hair at the back of his neck, the feel of him already familiar again.

A chime sounded overhead, followed by an announcement from the pilot regarding takeoff. The plane taxied down the runway, picking up speed.

"Play more?" Jack sketched his fingertips down her cheek, igniting a fluttering heat in her belly. "That might be the first time anyone has ever suggested that a Murphy male didn't play enough. You realize we're going to see a hockey game?"

She knew he was referring to the nonstop contests that had gone on at the Murphy household when they were younger. Speed skating on the homemade hockey pond at one end of the backyard. Swimming races in the pool. Tug-of-war battles where the whole neighborhood took sides.

"I'm not talking about that kind of play." Her admission coincided with their liftoff, and Alicia couldn't say which one made her heart lurch more.

Pinned to her seat by the speed of the aircraft, she felt mesmerized by Jack's green eyes as he watched her.

"This isn't a long flight," he reminded her, though his hand already drifted down her neck, his fingers skimming her collarbone and just beneath the edge of her simple white blouse. "We'll only be in the air for a short time."

Her nerve endings danced under his touch, as if all feeling was concentrated wherever his hands went. She arched in her seat, defying the force of gravity to be closer to the source of the pleasurable sensations.

"I think we can still have some fun." The tingled humming along her skin spread to the tops of her breasts, the sweet ache moving through her. "Haven't you ever heard of a quickie?"

"Do you know how hard men strive *not* to be quick about sex?" His palm stilled over the lace of her bra. The heat in his eyes singed her.

Electrified her. The buzz traveled from her breasts to her womb, warming her sex until she squirmed in her seat.

"Surely you could make an exception, just this once."

One minute she was pining for his touch, urging him to take her in the small, private cabin. The next he had her out of her seat belt and hoisted in his arms. He charged through the plane to the big leather sofa in back, dropping her gently onto the buttery-soft surface. Above her, he peeled off his jacket and the black T-shirt he wore beneath it. He jammed a finger to a button on the panel overhead, dimming the lights throughout the cabin. His hands went for the buckle on his pants before he even lay down, drawing her gaze to the bulge beneath his fly.

"I guess that's a yes," she mused, tugging a creamy chenille afghan closer as she watched him undress the rest of the way.

Naked, he was a sight to behold. Layers of muscle roped together, every inch of him sleekly molded into a perfect male specimen. She didn't have long to look, however, before he fell on her with a hunger that surprised her. He feasted on her mouth and neck, drugging her with thorough kisses that left her breathless, while his hands made fast work of removing her clothes.

Beneath her, the plane engines droned and vibrated, drowning out everything but Jack as he rolled on a condom and stretched over her, his big body covering hers completely. The ache between her legs turned sharp, her hips arching to get closer to him. He answered by spreading her thighs with one of his own, providing a counterpressure to the sweet need inside her.

He cupped her bottom, drawing her to him without entering her. Her breasts pebbled tight against his chest until he edged away enough to take one in his mouth, suckling her hard. She rode his thigh, her sex slick and so ready for him that she reached between them to circle his erection with her hand. Gently at first. Then harder. Firmer.

The growl in his throat warned her she wouldn't have to wait for him much longer. He gripped her hand, halting her movements and prying her fingers free.

Being submissive was deliciously easy when she realized how much her touch affected him. Besides, she wanted him inside her when he came. Needed that connection with him.

"Ally." He grasped her wrists and trapped them against the sofa above her head. Staring down at her for a long moment, he positioned his hips just right to...

"O-o-h!" she cried when he entered her, the sensation so incredible she wanted it to last forever. But each moment of satisfaction led to new hunger, the sensual need spiraling higher and higher with every long, slow thrust of Jack's hips.

The pleasure built. Coiled. Tensed. Built some more. He worked her so thoroughly, so fervently that when he released her wrists to wrap her in his arms, she couldn't move, her body paralyzed by pleasure and anticipation of what would come next. An orgasm waited, so close. She wanted it desperately and at the same time didn't want it to ever arrive. Being here like this with Jack was the most perfect time she could ever remember.

What if they could be like this always?

A starburst exploded behind her eyes right before release hit her. Her body contracted, squeezing him tight, again and again. She arched into him, hauling him closer to ride the wave of sensations with her. He followed right behind her, his hips straining against hers.

Filling her.

Alicia lost track of time, tangled with him in the aftermath. The big leather couch fit both of them easily. At some point she covered them with the chenille afghan to ward off the chill of the plane's air-conditioning.

Jack was as quiet as her afterward. Because he'd been shaken by the connection they'd found again so quickly? Or because he wasn't ready for the feelings lovemaking could inspire? She didn't know. She wasn't sure she could answer those questions for herself, let alone him. She had no idea what was happening between her and Jack, but whatever it was, the magnetic force was too strong for her to ignore, too difficult to turn away from.

When the quiet began to worry her, she dropped a kiss on his shoulder.

"You have a real way with a quickie," she confided, hoping to move things to lighter, more manageable terrain.

"I want to make you happy." The words felt genuine and deep compared to her flip flirtation.

Her throat burned at the sincerity in his eyes. She tried to swallow past it and couldn't. Only a few days of having Jack back in her life and he'd sucked her in like quicksand—so deep that she wasn't sure she'd get away.

She wasn't sure she even wanted to.

"You do," she admitted, hoarseness in her voice betraying more than she was comfortable sharing. "Thank you for bringing me to Montreal."

She hadn't realized until she saw him again how much she'd missed him. How unfinished things had felt between them. Moreover, maybe she'd needed some time to play, too. She'd been working so hard on achieving her dreams—saving every dollar to buy an inn she could call her own—that she hadn't spent much time relaxing and having fun.

Before he could respond, the tone chimed again on the plane's PA system and the pilot made an announcement about landing. Over her shoulder, Alicia could see the city of Montreal below them. The Saint Lawrence Seaway snaked alongside the buildings, a myriad of bridges stretched out like tentacles across it.

They both wanted tonight to be all about enjoying each other—no business—and Jack seemed determined to deliver. But as her heart thawed like a creek in spring, Alicia wondered how she would survive a night of Jack Murphy at his most attentive and charming. Without the barriers of business and the future to shore up her defenses, she ran the risk of falling in love all over again.

11

AN HOUR LATER, Jack passed Alicia her ticket for their rink-side seats while he lingered with his youngest brother for a few more minutes. They'd been able to visit with Kyle and Axel briefly before the match, hanging out with them while they had their skates sharpened and personally taped their sticks. But now, as Kyle headed toward the locker room, Alicia took her leave and Axel was called into a meeting with one of the trainers.

Jack didn't bristle too much when she hugged his brother goodbye. After all, Alicia had been friends with Kyle and Axel before Jack had met her. But damn. His feelings toward her were as possessive now as they had been when they'd been dating. Possibly more so. What was wrong with him?

"Geez, bro. Do you have to wear your heart on your sleeve like a neon sign?" Kyle observed as Alicia walked away, her golden-blond hair brushing her lower back in tousled waves she hadn't quite tamed after they'd made love on the plane.

Still, Jack couldn't pull his gaze from her. Another player held a door for her as she walked out of the secured corridor where the team prepared for the game. The guy—a defenseman who towered over her—didn't quite drool as she passed, but the bastard's eyes followed her almost as long as Jack's did.

"I don't know what you're talking about." He pinned the defenseman with a steady look after the other player lumbered to a bench in front of his locker.

No sense letting the Russian behemoth think that Alicia was available.

Only a handful of guys had made it into the locker room so far, most of them still busy prepping their equipment for the game. And the locker room wasn't some sweaty, tile-covered cave like in high school. Here, the visiting team could hang out comfortably on padded leather benches, with carpets on the floor and the walls painted and decorated with clippings from highlight moments in the National Hockey League. The players didn't really even undress at this point, since they still had on some of the gear from their morning skate. They spent more time taping thumbs or ankles, noses or hands, depending on what body part they'd broken most recently in a notoriously rough sport. Hell, they had a doctor on call for intermission stitches.

Today, Kyle's broken nose wasn't taped, but his two black eyes were witness enough to the injury. One eye was bloodshot from a broken vessel. But he blended well enough with the rest of his team, the whole group a mass of scrapes, bruises and crooked noses.

The players weren't all that different from the guys in Jack's unit back in the navy. They were battle-scarred and seasoned, working in tandem for a common goal.

Kyle waved his hand in front of Jack's face, distracting him from the "don't go there" vibe he was sending his brother's teammate for good measure.

"You with me, Jack?" Kyle asked, a grin tipping one slightly swollen cheek. "Because I'm not going to help you out if you get Oleg pissed off."

"Right. Sorry." He shook his head, bringing himself back to the conversation. He tried to remember what his brother had said to him…. Oh, yeah. Heart on his sleeve. "I'm back where I left off with her four years ago. It's the damnedest thing. I walked away back then, determined to give her some space to be her own person and enjoy college without me hovering over her. But the first time I see her—bam! She's in my head all the time."

Kyle studied his knuckles as he wound athletic tape between his fingers. "Does she know?"

"Know what? That I'm crazy about her?" Jack shrugged. "She's still trying to get past what happened when we broke up. Being left out of the loop about Cristina and the kidnapping didn't go over so well."

He'd come to regret the way he'd handled the situation back then. But he could do better with Alicia this time. He just had to figure out how to convince her to give him a second chance, to win her trust again. Not just for tonight, but forever.

His brother nodded and ripped the tape with his

teeth. "She was having a rough semester that spring after you left. Her father was pressuring her to ditch Boston College. She quit freelancing for Dad even though she really liked the job. And you know, as much as the Murphy family drama can bug us, I think Alicia sort of liked hanging out at the house on the weekends."

Jack reached into Kyle's open locker and grabbed the elbow pads and shin guards he'd need next. "Our family drama doesn't seem so bad when you compare it to hers, with a pushy dad and a know-it-all brother who never had time for her. At least we're there for each other when it counts."

"Yeah, I felt like crap when I heard she had no one at that last meet, when she won two national titles." Kyle frowned, shaking his head. "I'd like to think that if I make it to the Stanley Cup playoffs, there'll be a few family members in the crowd. It's gotta suck when you don't have anyone to share that stuff."

Picturing all the other swimmers hugging their loved ones while Alicia went back to the locker room alone sent a shaft of pain through Jack's chest. He should have been honest with her about why he went into the navy. Why he didn't want to tie her down as a junior in college. It might not have made his leaving any easier on her, but at least she would have known that he didn't take off because he didn't care. Far from it. He'd gone because he cared too much, too soon.

"That's why I keep hoping she'll change her mind about moving to Bar Harbor. At least in Chatham she has friends and a thriving business with loyal customers. And she'd have *him,* assuming she gave him another chance to be a part of her life.

Kyle strapped on the shin guards as more players began to filter in. Some greeted each other with laughing insults, while the more intense players went straight to work getting dressed for the game. Jack knew he only had a few more minutes with his brother. The coach would want to talk to the assembled team soon.

And Jack didn't want to leave Alicia alone for too long on a night that was supposed to be all about her having a good time.

"Don't assume you know what's best for her." Kyle took the elbow pads from Jack's hands. "If she says she wants out of Chatham, you might want to respect that she knows her own mind."

"I do." Didn't he? "I just think it can't hurt to be sure. To understand why you're doing something so that it's not just a knee-jerk reaction."

Maybe part of him still believed she wanted to leave Cape Cod only because he had returned home.

"Think about it, Jack. She's had four years to figure out what she wants to do with her life. Four years to save enough money to buy this place. Her leaving town isn't just about you."

The reminder was enough to make Jack weigh the benefits of straightening out his brother's broken nose for him. One good swipe in the other direction, maybe?

It was all the conversation they had time to exchange before the coach stalked into the room with a clipboard under his arm, obviously ready to address the team.

Jack saw his cue to leave, and with a slap on his brother's chest pads for luck, he ducked out of the locker area. He was so preoccupied processing Kyle's suggestion that he didn't even bother giving Oleg the hairy eyeball on his way out.

Jack walked through the two sets of double doors that secured the visiting-team area, and went to find Alicia. He'd been so busy trying to win her back and save her from incurring any problems with the run-down property in Maine that he hadn't thought about how much this dream meant to her.

By pointing out all the inn's flaws would he be no better than her father, who—in his desire to "help" his daughter—refused to consider what made Alicia happy? As Jack hurried down the final set of stairs to the rink-level seats, he spied Alicia, now decked out in Boston Bears gear. She'd bought a jersey and a baseball cap with the team logo to show her support.

She didn't hesitate to support other people in their aspirations. For all Jack knew, maybe she'd have understood his need to go into the navy, to follow a calling that felt right to him. No way would he yank the rug out from under her when she'd never known the feeling of having someone in her corner, cheering her on through it all.

He would find a way to be there for her now, when she was working so hard to achieve a dream. So what if the bed-and-breakfast needed a lot of capital before it started earning a profit? He'd invested in businesses all over Cape Cod to help local entrepreneurs. Why not invest in Alicia?

Decision made, he didn't slide into the seat beside her. Instead, he turned on his heel to make a call in private—away from the noise of the arena crowd. He had a lot to take care of if he was going to pull off the plan taking shape in his head. But for Alicia—for a shot at a future—he'd do whatever it took.

MIDWAY THROUGH THE THIRD period, Alicia noticed that Jack had already checked out of his brother's game. Granted, it was preseason, and these early matches weren't of major importance. But even so, did he have to read a text message for the third time?

"Did you see Kyle's hat trick?" she asked, leaning close.

"What?" Jack straightened so fast he almost dropped the phone he'd been using. Frowning as he looked out onto the ice, he realized pretty quickly that she'd been messing with him.

Tough to score a hat trick when he wasn't even out skating. The players went on in shifts and Kyle had sat down about two minutes prior. Axel was still on the ice, but looking toward the bench since he was due to switch out. The Murphy clan's honorary brother was a defensive powerhouse and his arrival on the Boston team had been much heralded in the media.

"Okay, you caught me. Kyle still has two goals, not three. But your attention has wandered enough that it makes a woman doubt her appeal." She nodded toward the phone resting on Jack's knee, while the crowd cheered a hard check into the boards nearby.

The players smashed into the glass, one guy's face distorted as he slid down the barrier.

"I apologize." Jack shut the phone in mid message. "I can finish this up later."

"I don't mean to take you away from something important." In fact, she really hoped it was urgent if he was spending time playing with technology instead of being with her.

Otherwise, what did that say about her own level of importance in his life?

"It's not a big deal," he assured her, not realizing that might actually be more hurtful. "I can delay delivering Keith's boat for only so long, so I'd rather spend the remaining time with you than straightening out a business transaction." He tapped the case of his phone for emphasis.

"Are you investing in another bar?" Curiosity got the best of her and she had to ask.

"You could say I'm helping a struggling business, yes." And with that cryptic answer, he wrapped an arm around her as the crowd in the arena broke into shouts and catcalls.

"They're fighting," Alicia observed, when she turned her attention back to the ice.

Sure enough, a mammoth defenseman on the Montreal team had one of Kyle's teammates in a headlock. Gloves were coming off all over the rink as other players got involved. Even skaters from the bench were emerging onto the ice, everyone prepared to join in the skirmish.

The linesmen watched, but weren't pulling men off each other yet. Kyle went out into the thick of things along with two other guys who skated in his line.

"Damn! And it's only the preseason. Can you imagine what this rivalry will be like by the time the playoffs roll around?" Jack asked Alicia, sounding disgusted as one player socked another, backing him into the boards.

"I don't mind hockey fights," she admitted, knowing the comment would sound more bloodthirsty than how she meant it.

Predictably, Jack's brows soared up to his hairline for a moment.

"Who knew you had a violent streak?" He grinned. "But you're not alone in liking the fights. That's why the league doesn't outlaw them altogether."

Finally, the linesmen stepped in to slow things down. Kyle seemed to be holding his own with a player from the other team who'd tried to stick up for his buddy.

"I don't like it for the violence," she clarified. "And I hate seeing anyone get hurt. But there's something open and honest about admitting you're pissed off and acting on it. It's fast and primitive, but at least it's genuine. In a world full of superficial sentiment, where we're conditioned never to cause a stir, there's something cathartic about occasionally acting on your feelings."

As order was slowly restored, penalties were assigned to both teams and the play continued, four on four. Kyle came out on the ice again during a shift change, and Jack waved a towel with the Boston Bears team colors.

"Do you feel that you don't get to express yourself with your dad?" He sat forward in his seat for the face-off as the ref dropped the puck to restart the game.

"Sort of. My dad speaks his mind. The problem is that he doesn't appreciate anyone else—especially someone who disagrees with him—speaking theirs." She flinched as two players crashed into the boards right in front of them, their bodies slamming the Plexi-glas so hard it shook. "Not that his preferences stop me from saying what I want, but I can disagree with him all day long and he doesn't really hear it. He forges ahead with what he wants, anyhow."

"No wonder you like my family," Jack acknowl-edged. "It's a nonstop mission to one-up each other. I always found it fairly juvenile, but at least we're con-tinually talking to one another—if only for the sake of running our mouths."

"You *are* a mouthy group." She jumped to her feet as Kyle scored his third goal of the night.

The hat trick—three goals scored by the same player in a single game—prompted fans all over the arena to do more than "tip their caps." They threw their hats out onto the ice to honor the scorer, a tradition maintained even for a player on a visiting team.

Alicia tossed her baseball cap in a slow-pitch softball arc so it would fly up and over the protective boards surrounding the rink. She'd bought it to show her sup-port for Kyle anyhow, so it seemed only fitting to send the hat out onto the ice now. Cleanup crews would have to pick up all the headgear before play continued, and the rink would donate them to a local charity.

When she'd cheered herself hoarse and found her seat again, she felt Jack's palm envelop hers and squeeze.

"Ally." His voice warmed her ear, his mouth closer than she'd expected.

The combination of sound and heat sent a pleasant shiver through her.

"Mmm?" She wondered if the plane ride back would be as much fun as the trip here. Already, her body tingled at the suggestion of intimacy.

"I'm sorry I wasn't there when you won at the national-championship meet."

His words were so unexpected, so genuinely full of regret, they chased away the sensual thrill curling inside her.

"What made you think of that?" She'd blocked that time from her mind, the final meet a bittersweet win when she'd had no one to share it with. Sure, it was nice to win with her teammates, but while they were all mobbed by family, friends and significant others, Alicia had wandered back to the locker room alone.

"This." He gestured to the arena full of fans who'd cheered for Kyle Murphy's first hat trick at the NHL level. "Eighteen thousand people celebrating a player's talent and accomplishment. You should have had that your junior year, when you were a two-event winner instead of…"

Instead of informing her dad by email that she'd won.

His reply had been full of reminders that swimming would never lead to a real career, though he'd managed a "congratulations" at the end of the note. The memory sparked a surprising burn in Alicia's throat, especially with the hum of energy still infusing the Montreal arena after the impromptu tribute to Kyle.

"Sports aren't everything." She'd reminded herself of that often, trying to keep the season and the win in perspective.

"But you worked your butt off to be the best and you deserved to have someone there who knew exactly how tough it was to achieve what you did." Jack reached over to graze her cheek with his knuckles. "I always admired how hard you worked to accomplish your goals."

Surprised by the admission and his apology, she nodded, mute with emotion for a moment. She hadn't expected Jack to think back about that day, especially after she'd learned what he'd been going through during the weeks leading up to the championship meet he'd missed. So it meant a lot—even all these years later— to know he'd been proud of her.

"Thank you," she finally murmured, leaning across the hard metal arm of the stadium seat to kiss his cheek. "I missed you that day."

The warmth in her heart was more than attraction or awareness. It went deeper than that, reaching a place inside her no one else had touched since her breakup with Jack. Despite her best intentions, she knew she was in love with this man all over again.

Could he be apologizing for the past now because he

wanted a future with her, after all? Hope beat fiercely in her heart. Maybe Jack was ready to be open and honest with her, to let her share in his life in a way that he hadn't been prepared for four years earlier. Back then, he'd walked away rather than confiding in her. He'd made the decision to join the navy, which affected them both deeply, without ever asking for her opinion. He'd just broken up with her—no explanations, no arguments.

Perhaps his apology today was an olive branch that could lead toward a different kind of future. A future where they might not only confide in each other, but argue back and forth without worrying about pushing the other away. For a couple of strong personalities like them, that seemed important. Comforting.

Even if it meant returning to the Cape and forsaking the dream of the inn on the Maine coast, Alicia wanted to think about a future with Jack. As long as she could be his partner and not someone he informed of his choices after he made them, she was on board. Because after four years of keeping her eyes peeled for a man she'd want in her life, she'd never met anyone who came close to Jack Murphy.

12

ACTIONS SPOKE LOUDER than words, right?

The next morning, Jack was damn pleased with himself—he was going to pull off an action that would surprise Alicia to her toenails. He had a contract for the Bar Harbor property in one hand and a list of repairs he thought they should make within the first year in the other. He'd even gotten cost estimates on the repairs and made a timetable for when and how the work could be completed.

Alicia would be thrilled, her dream come true facilitated by the kind of capital that would take the property from ramshackle charm to high functionality for her guests. Better yet, it would be a task they could tackle together. She hadn't thought he supported her idea of starting a business in Maine. But she would see how serious he was about making a commitment to the property—to her—when he gave her the signed contract for the inn she'd poured so much thought into with her sketches and plans.

He had been up half the night after they returned from Montreal, working to make it happen. Alicia had spent the night on the boat with him, and he'd returned to the inn at dawn, before she awoke, so he could have the sale contract signed by the owner. Without a Realtor or a bank involved, the process was actually very simple and straightforward. The owner had been elated at the prospect of a cash sale, even knocking a substantial amount off his asking price when Jack presented him with a list of the flaws he'd found in the structure.

Now, seated on the deck of Keith's boat, Jack waited for Alicia to emerge from the cabin below. He'd heard the shower switch off about ten minutes earlier, so he knew the wait was almost over.

"Morning," she called as she reached the top step, stretching up on her toes and throwing her arms wide. "Isn't it beautiful out?"

A pair of soft, well-worn jeans showcased her hips, while a pink cotton sweater kept her warm against the slight nip of fall in the air. She'd dried her long hair enough to take the worst of the dampness out, but he guessed her head must feel cool in the morning breeze. As usual, no makeup hid her pretty features. She looked beautiful to him, a vision he'd love to see every day.

But he kept that sentiment to himself. He didn't want that kind of pressure mixed up in a gift he wanted to give her no matter how she felt about him.

"Beautiful," he agreed, unable to take his eyes off her to assess the scenery.

"There are even a few trees turning red and yellow."

She pointed toward the shore as she closed the distance between them, her feet silent on the deck in a pair of leather moccasins.

"Fall comes early up here." Even a few hours north of where they'd grown up made a big difference, and despite the fact that it was still summer, fall was starting to creep in around the edges.

Would he get to share the season with her this year? Other years? A chill of foreboding chased down his spine and he wasn't sure why. He'd worked too hard to make this moment right for her to mess it up now.

He would simply offer up the property as an olive branch for the past and be done with it. If she wanted more from him on a personal level, she knew where to find him. He didn't want her to feel as if his investment in the inn was tied to any expectation of a relationship.

"Speaking of early—" she wound her way across the deck to stand beside him at the rail "—you must have gone out at the crack of dawn."

"You noticed." He thought for sure she'd been sleeping. "Miss me?"

"I missed a few things while you were gone." She sidled closer and threaded her arms around his waist, resting a hand on his hip.

Damn, but he had missed her, too. He hadn't let himself think about how much until he was out of the navy for good. Once, during a family July Fourth ball game that coincided with his leave, he'd peered over at the pitcher's mound in the backyard and known she should have been there. For one thing, she would have brought her A-game and goaded everyone on the opposite team just for fun. More importantly, she would have flat-out enjoyed the day. The family. The fun. He'd known then that he'd screwed up with her. But by that point she'd been dating someone else.

"Good to know my finer qualities are appreciated." Wrapping her in his arms, he reeled her close to hold her tight, savoring the surprise he had in store for her.

The waves splashed against the hull, but the boat was nice and steady despite the choppy water. He'd made plans to meet Keith's CFO in a couple hours, unable to stall the handoff of the watercraft any longer. Alicia had already arranged for a rental car to be dropped off for her at the bed-and-breakfast, so she could explore the Bar Harbor area a little more before returning home.

"Should I sit down for your assessment of the property?" Edging back, she gazed up at him and shielded her eyes from the glare of the sun on the water. Although it wasn't hot, it was a bright, clear day. "I'll admit I'm a little nervous about going over that big list I spotted on your phone yesterday."

That was the opening he'd been waiting for. His chance to make things right with Alicia.

He'd played this out a few different ways in his head in the early hours of morning, unsure how to proceed. A damn foreign feeling for him, since he'd been born sure of himself. Now that the time had arrived to reveal what he'd done, he felt all the more pressure to get it right.

"Maybe that's a good idea." He looked around the

dock and up to the rambling building, his gaze coming to rest on the two Adirondack chairs closest to the water, near the fire pit. "Let's go sit there."

Nodding, she followed him off the boat and down the planked pier to the big wooden seats, whose bright paint had faded to sun-washed shades.

"You really hate the house, don't you?" she asked as she sank into her chair, her brown eyes studying him. "You think it's past the point of no return."

"No." He reached for his phone, thinking it would be quicker to simply show her the list so she understood some of his rationale for investing in the property. "But it's priced too high when you consider some of the major repairs that need to be made."

Pulling up the notepad feature, he handed the device to her, giving her time to absorb the problems.

Alicia whistled softly between her teeth. "These are serious setbacks." Her finger flicked down the touch screen, scrolling through his notes. "The roof alone would cost—wow. You projected the costs, too?"

Frowning, she stilled her finger on the screen, and Jack tried to remember if he'd made some notes about the sale at the bottom of the page. Or had he put that information in another file? He'd crammed a lot of research into a couple of days, so his brain was still swimming with numbers. He didn't want to ruin the surprise.

"I thought it might help you to have some rough figures to work with." He reached to retrieve the cell. "But the bottom line is this—"

When she didn't hand it over, he tugged the phone from her fingers.

"It's a bad investment," she said.

At the same time, he announced, "I bought it for you."

ALICIA MUST HAVE FORGOTTEN to breathe.

Her world stilled. Narrowed to the news Jack had just dropped on her like a neutron bomb. Had he really just said that he'd bought the bed-and-breakfast?

"I'm sorry." She blinked to clear the pandemonium in her mind. Forced herself to take a breath. "What did you say?"

Jamming the cell phone in the pocket of his cargo shorts, Jack shifted on the seat beside her, his knee grazing hers.

"I said I bought this place." He gestured to the sprawling three-story structure behind them, the grand home fallen on hard times that she'd been dreaming about bringing back to life. "All the problems that I listed need to be addressed, so it won't be easy to turn this property into a profitable, thriving business. But I know how much it means to you and I know how committed you are to doing this."

His hand covered hers where it rested on the wide wooden arm of the Adirondack chair. Birds chirped in the silence while he waited for her to say something, but she couldn't begin to process what all of it meant. *He'd* bought *her* property? She watched a squirrel shamble across the yard and up a tall oak tree.

"Is it a new acquisition for Murphy Resorts?" She knew his father wanted her to come back to work for the company. Was this some kind of Murphy maneuver to ensure she returned to the corporate fold?

The thought of her charming seaside inn turned into a homogenized, vanilla hotel made her heart feel hollow. Didn't Jack understand what she wanted better than that?

"No." He shook his head, his voice adamant. "*I* invested in this place. My father's company isn't involved. I wanted you to be able to follow your heart and make the kind of life for yourself that you dream about. I know I haven't been very supportive of the move to Bar Harbor. But I didn't understand how hard you've worked to make this place a reality. I realize how much your family has stood in your way, and you deserve the chance to spread your wings."

He withdrew a sheaf of papers from his pocket. Folded and stiff, the sheets crinkled as he smoothed them so she could read the writing. Through the haze of her confusion, she could see a sales contract with the former owner's name scrawled next to Jack's.

She hadn't believed her ears, but she couldn't doubt her eyes. What she couldn't understand was why he would do something like this. Heat crawled up the back of her neck, making her itchy and uncomfortable. The day that had seemed so beautiful and full of possibilities a little while ago now felt suffocating.

"You think it will help me 'spread my wings' by handing me the property I wanted to buy myself?" She tugged at the neckline of her hooded sweater, unable to get enough air. "I'm not sure how I can feel the fulfillment of realizing a dream if it arrives gift-wrapped on a silver platter. Why would you swoop in and steal this moment from me? Do you think I'm too feebleminded or weak to have haggled for a better price? Or found another property?"

She could tell that her words had been harsh by the way his shoulders tensed. His hand slid away from where it had rested on her forearm. But how else could she describe what he'd done?

"I wanted to help you bring the property into the black faster. The list of repairs is so long and expensive they would have been cost prohibitive if you used your start-up cash to buy the inn. This way, you can afford the repairs and open for business by spring. Generating operating income will give you a fighting chance to make the business profitable."

"And because you know best, you bought the place without even discussing it with me." Memories of all the times her father had made decisions for her swamped her. Why had she thought Jack was any different? "Just like when you broke up with me for my own good. You planned the end of our relationship and executed it, all without any input from me. So why ask me for my opinion on how to handle the purchase of the bed-and-breakfast that I've been dreaming about and planning for?"

She heard the unsteadiness in her voice and hated the quavering tone. But after the time they'd spent together, she'd thought they were growing closer. No. Worse than that, she'd fallen in love with him all over again, only to be confronted with how foolish she'd been. Again.

Jack knew best. Then and now.

"I didn't do it to take the decision out of your hands." He stood, pacing around the fire pit like a caged animal looking for a way out. His feet crunched over fallen twigs and pine needles. "Hell, anyone could see you'd made up your mind to buy the place long before you even set out for Maine. I knew when I saw that damn notebook of yours with the plans for a cabana and the diagram for a beach bungalow that this was a done deal. I thought I was doing you a favor because..."

He paused. His green eyes flashed to hers with fiery heat.

"Because why?" She rose, feeling the tension in the air.

Had he bought the inn for any reason other than he-man protectiveness? Did any sentimentality lurk underneath the assurance that he knew what was best for everyone around him?

"Because I had faith in your vision, and you work harder than anyone I know," he admitted finally. The words were quieter than the rest of his heated diatribe, as if they'd come from deeper down inside him. "You deserve this chance, Alicia."

The anger seeped out of her as he stared her down, daring her to argue. She wouldn't. Not now. She couldn't remain mad at someone who believed in her—possibly the only person in the world who would make that claim. Jack *was* different from her father. And he hadn't simply bought the inn to keep her from fighting her own battles. He wanted to help, and she couldn't hold that against him.

Yet, she realized as she wavered on her feet, she had hoped for a lot more from Jack. Her limbs felt like wrung-out dishrags, her whole body sapped of the anger and conviction she'd felt just moments ago. Jack hadn't done any of this because he wanted to be with her or start a future here beside her. There was no mention of the old feelings they had once shared. Sinking back into her chair, she tried to come to terms with what that meant.

"I'm sorry," she murmured, the words raw in her throat, which suddenly burned with unspoken emotions. "I'm being ungrateful when you've been thoughtful and generous. I—" She had to stop and clear her throat. And, oh, God, what was the matter with her? "I will pay you back as soon as I can start generating some income and work out a budget. You know I'm good for it."

She tried to paste on a game face, but could tell it wasn't quite coming together. Jack remained on his feet on the other side of the fire pit, watching her.

Slowly, he nodded. "I know. And it was probably a bad idea to surprise you with something so important. I don't know what I was thinking. I was caught up in how excited you were about the whole thing."

Okay, now she felt like a huge ogre. A good friend would throw herself at his mercy and beg for forgiveness for being such an ingrate, except she didn't want to be just a good friend. She wanted so much more, and he…

He was currently checking his watch.

"I should really be shoving off if I'm going to meet Keith's buddy." He stuffed his hands in his pockets. "I know you're renting a car and checking out the area, but maybe when you come back to Chatham, we could get together. I can help you with the move."

Again, her eyes flew to his, searching. Hoping. Because she was foolish like that. But his gaze remained guarded, assuring her he was offering the help only to be nice. Because they were *friends,* apparently. Friends with too many damn benefits.

And for crying out loud, hadn't it hurt enough to have him walk away once? She would be an idiot of the first order if she kept putting herself in a position to experience the unique sting of that particular heartache.

"Sounds great," she lied, knowing she wouldn't call him until it was time to pay the first installment of the massive loan he'd forced upon her by buying the inn. "I appreciate your faith in me. I will make sure it's well placed."

She had no idea where the stilted words originated from. She felt like a parrot on autoplay, mindlessly speaking phrases with little real meaning. Who would have thought this day would find her relationship with him relegated to the same importance as the connection he shared with the bar owners he'd financed back on the Cape? Jack and she now had a business arrangement. Nothing more. Nothing less.

Neither of them moved for a long moment. Finally, Jack broke the standoff and approached her, his arms open. Alicia thought it would be healthiest to step back, to refrain from feeling his strong, warm body against hers. But after all they'd shared, she discovered she didn't have the willpower to deny the embrace.

Stepping into his arms, she laid her cheek on his chest. Felt the steady thrum of his heartbeat there. How could she have read everything so wrong these last few days? Yet, if ever there was a time to declare feelings for her, it would be now. Jack would say something now.

The beat of his pulse drummed in one ear while the chirping of birds and the wash of waves along the shore sounded in the other.

"Call me," he reminded her, kissing the top of her head. Cupping the base of her skull and threading his fingers into her hair.

Just before she melted, she stepped back. Nodding.

"Of course." At last she managed to mask her emotions, a trick she'd perfected that day at the championships, when no one was there to see her moment of triumph. "Travel safe. And thank you."

With that, he was gone.

Her eyes followed his progress down the grass and onto the pier. Onto Keith's forty-five-foot power catamaran that could practically drive itself. Jack flipped the engine on and engaged the self-steering mechanism to back away from the dock. The boat seemed to surgically remove itself from its moorings, much like Jack neatly extricated himself from her life and a chance reunion that was never meant to be.

Lifting her hand to wave goodbye, she congratulated herself on putting on a good front. Right up until the tears broke through the dam as he cruised out of sight.

13

"YOU JUST TOOK OFF?"

Jack realized the story sounded stupid in the retelling. But his brother Danny hadn't been standing there with him and Alicia. He didn't know how prickly Alicia LeBlanc could be about accepting help. About maintaining independence.

And Jack sure as hell still didn't understand how to be what this woman needed.

He'd been back in Chatham for all of three days, trying to figure out his next move with Alicia—assuming he even had one. Somehow he'd ended up at his parents' house, since he couldn't sleep on the *Vesta* now that Keith had it. He and Keith had exchanged a few messages since Keith had taken the sailboat for a week. He'd apparently found an interior decorator aboard the *Vesta* the night after Ryan's engagement party. As if Jack would ever hire anyone to lay a finger on the vintage sailboat. But the woman had misread the slip numbers on the pier, and next thing Keith knew, he was out to sea with a stranger.

Jack had sent his brother ten different messages asking him not to sell the boat. After realizing that he still had feelings for Alicia—no, damn it, that he *loved* her—he didn't want to get rid of it. Not yet.

Which brought him back to the conversation with the second-youngest Murphy brother, Danny, over brandy on the back porch just past sunset.

"Bro? You in there?" Danny wadded up a cocktail napkin and pegged him in the temple with it. "Why the hell would you buy her a million-dollar property and then run for the hills? Are you trying to mess with her mind, or do you get off on playing hard to get?"

His brother was younger than him by three years, but Jack had related to Dan more than any of the others since long before their mutual decision to enter the navy. Not that their similarities helped them get along. Danny was the crustiest of the bunch, unwilling to embroider the truth for any reason whatsoever, determined to live by his own light and consequences be damned. There was a grounded quality to him that Jack appreciated.

"No." Jack tossed the napkin back, taking dead-center aim at his brother's beak. "Don't you have any sense of tact? I couldn't make a big play for her the moment I purchased the inn. How tasteless would that be? She'd think I was trying to buy her affection."

Although, maybe she would have thought differently if he'd told her that he loved her. It had been tough enough to admit it to himself and face up to the magnitude of the mistake he'd made four years ago. But now he'd compounded the error by not telling her how he felt.

He hadn't thought the whole thing through well enough when he'd bought the bed-and-breakfast. That was the main problem. He'd been so determined to help her achieve her goals—unwilling to undermine what she wanted, the way her old man had—that he'd moved too fast and hadn't considered the consequences. That was totally unlike him. But it showed how much she affected him.

Still, he hadn't felt right asking to be a part of her life when she'd been reeling with the news that he'd bought the old inn.

"No wonder she isn't speaking to you." Dan gulped the rest of his brandy, settling his work boots on the railing where he and Jack looked out over the Atlantic. He ran his fingers over the scruffy goatee he'd been sporting for the past year. "I'd cut you off, too, if you shipped out right when things were starting to get interesting. Especially since you did that to the same girl once before. Am I remembering that right?"

Jack slammed his drink down on the wrought-iron table between them. He hadn't told his brother the more intimate details of his reunion with Alicia, obviously, but he'd given the highlights, after Dan had hounded him about why he looked so down in the dumps.

"Don't go there." He jammed a finger in Dan's face, unwilling to listen to any more. "You know why I joined the navy."

He knew a moment's regret for even bringing it up when a shadow passed through his brother's eyes. Dan had been wrecked when Stephanie Rosen had been taken captive. The guy had always been a rebel, so Jack was convinced he'd try to pull some lone-wolf vigilante crap if left to his own devices. No one else had known what Stephanie meant to Dan, but Jack had been in the city to see Danny's band the weekend they met.

He'd give his eyeteeth to know if his brother had tried to contact her since they'd returned home. Last he'd heard, Stephanie was still single, recovering from her ordeal through work at a counseling center. Dan was due to ship out again in six weeks.

"Free pass this time, bro, because I know you're in a bad place." Danny shot him a level look, a vein pulsing hard down the center of his forehead. "But you've got no excuses for letting her slip away. And I can tell you firsthand, the longer you wait to see her, the harder it's going to be...."

Dan plucked the brandy bottle from the floor and topped off their glasses.

Jack eased back in his chair, gaze fixed on the horizon, where the lights of a handful of boats blinked in the misty, late-summer evening. Danny might be messed in the head with his own love life, but his advice was sound. Jack had checked out on Alicia once before. How could he have done it a second time? Why hadn't he stuck around and talked it through even if that talk— or fight—had been tough?

That day, it had seemed like a good plan. He'd

thought he was being a stand-up guy, keeping his business offer separate from what he wanted from her personally. But he hadn't explained that to Alicia, falling into the same old dumb-ass thinking that he knew what was best.

"You're right." He set down the brandy and stood, wishing the *Vesta* was in its old slip at the marina so he could take off tonight. Then again, why not ring for a plane as he had when they'd gone to the hockey game? That would put him back in Bar Harbor before midnight. "I'm going to talk to her tonight. Now."

"Seriously?" Danny's feet slipped off the railing. "You're taking my advice?"

"Yes." He clapped his brother on the back. "You're not a head case all the time. Now and then, I could swear you know what you're talking about."

Jack grinned, liking his plan more and more by the minute. He would do what he should have done three days ago. Tell Alicia that he didn't just want to buy the damn inn for her. He wanted to be a part of the future she was building.

He just prayed it wasn't too late.

ADJUSTING THE CLOSED SIGN on the front door of the inn on her way out, Alicia took a cup of tea onto one of the wide, crooked porches that needed refurbishing. She'd spent the last few days roaming all over the property, doing an inventory with the help of a home inspector to catalog the work that needed attention. They had yet to set a closing date, but she was working on it. The seller was only too happy to let Alicia stay in one of the rooms, as long as she paid for the utilities.

After Jack had left, she'd found a copy of his list of projected repairs and costs in her email in-box. No note. No personal message. Just an orderly review that was more thorough than what she'd paid a professional for the day before. But wasn't that just like Jack? Smart. Efficient. Well suited to take charge and be a leader.

As she settled into a porch swing hung from sturdy rafters that hadn't shifted with the rest of the structure, Alicia wrapped her hands tighter around her mug in the cool night air, wondering how she'd repay Jack. Regardless of how she felt about what he'd done, she needed to send him some kind of business plan and a payment schedule. Too bad the renovations on the inn didn't feel as exciting without him in her life to share the project.

A neighbor must have lit a bonfire somewhere nearby, for the fragrant musk of burning fruitwood hung sweet in the air. Still, it couldn't mask the scent of the ocean, a briny smell that made her think of Jack and their time on the boat, and on the *Vesta* when they were dating. He was such a big part of her best memories.

Lifting her tea to her lips, she drank the blackberry-sage brew from a local tea shop. The flavorful drink didn't soothe her one bit. Her heart ached without Jack. The hollow pit in her chest reminded her that she should have fought harder for him. Should have yelled at him and argued with him about ditching her again. Maybe it would have been an exercise in embarrassment and futility, but then again, maybe not. They'd argued plenty of times over far less important things. Why not fight for each other? For something that mattered? She'd never really stood up to her father, and she hadn't truly stood up to Jack, either. She'd just let them walk away. She'd let the relationships fade because it was easier than a deeper confrontation that might have yielded results.

Why had she let her issues with her dad get in the way of how she felt about Jack? Jack was so much more openhearted than her father, which made it all the more tragic that she'd let her problems with her dad shut down her relationship with a great guy. Not a perfect guy, but a damn amazing one all the same.

She had half a mind to march into the Murphy house and issue a challenge to Jack. Winner take all; the stakes being a real relationship. Maybe she could suggest a windsurfing contest. She'd definitely beat him at windsurfing.

Alicia was so swept up in her visions of outdoing Jack and winning back a chance to be with him that she didn't realize someone was approaching the inn until she heard boot steps on the plank porch.

"Hello?" She jumped off the swing, sloshing her tea on the painted floor as she hurried to peer around the corner of the wraparound porch, where it extended along the west side of the inn.

Who would show up here so late? Someone seeking a room at the inn? Edging around a plant stand with a pot of heirloom tomatoes, she nearly slammed into the unexpected guest.

"Jack?"

Stunned to see him, she scrambled back, righting herself against a heavy support post.

Eyes adjusting to the shadows, she took in the familiar lines of his face. The softly worn leather jacket and jeans.

"Hello, Alicia." His voice hummed through her as if someone had started an engine inside her.

"What are you doing here?" She thought about her chaotic thoughts just moments before, risking all for a chance to be with him. Could she be so brazen? Put her heart on the line for a third time? But then, maybe she hadn't put anything on the line those other times.

Maybe she needed to risk everything so there would be absolutely no regrets. No room for self-doubt.

"I came back to tell you a few things I left out the last time we spoke."

"Did you drive up?" She arched up on her toes to see past him to the parking area in front.

"I flew, actually. Although I did rent a car after I got to the airport. When I realized how much I needed to see you, I didn't want to wait an extra minute." He gestured toward the porch swing, which was still swaying from when she'd jumped out of it. "Do you mind if we have a seat?"

He needed to see her? She realized she was trembling all over. Her nerves made her jittery inside and out. It occurred to her that he'd never sought her out before.

Not for his own sake. The first time he'd kissed her and asked her out, it had been the result of a dare from his older brother. Then, when they'd gotten together this time, it had been pure coincidence. Or maybe some romantic machinations on Keith's part. But either way, Jack hadn't been looking for her.

Alicia wanted to see what he had to say for himself when left to his own designs.

Setting her mug on the porch rail, she nodded toward the beach. "Could we walk down by the water instead?" She was way too nervous to sit.

The clean, crisp late-summer air would help steady her. The sound of the water rolling gently along the shore always soothed her. Besides, maybe it would help to be on more neutral ground than the porch of the house they'd already fought about.

He followed her down to the water. Out from under the canopy of pine trees, the night turned brighter. The full white face of the moon reflected on the bay in a long, liquid stream.

"I wasn't using my head when I bought the bed-and-breakfast," he started.

Her feet halted in the damp sand as her heart sank. "You want me to repay the loan already?"

"No." He shook his head and she could see the strain in his eyes as he searched for words. "Not at all. Wow, I'm not cut out for this."

She shifted from one foot to the other, suddenly chilled. Still, she remained silent, determined to find out what could have incited him to take a plane to see her on the spur of the moment.

"What I meant was, I wish I'd consulted you first. I see now that you've put up with a lot of maneuvering from your family in the past, and it would have been better to discuss the purchase with you instead of trying to make a big gesture."

She took in the words, letting them roll through her as she absorbed the sincerity in his eyes. She wanted to tell him she understood, that she'd had an idea for fighting through this together, but he cut her off.

"Wait." His determined look told her he had more to say. "I just want you to know that I understand I screwed up. But I'd like to think I'm smart enough to learn from my mistakes. Can you forgive me?"

"It's okay." She tugged her feet out of the damp sand and used the toe of her sneaker to fill in the depression where she'd stood. "I had my heart set on this property, so even if you told me the roof was caving in, I would have found a way to buy it and fix it up. You just… caught me off guard when you bought the place. Sometimes I've felt like you were being overprotective, and I thought this might be your way of assuring I didn't fall on my face."

"I don't doubt for a minute your ability to turn this inn around. I just wanted it to be something you could enjoy instead of something stressful. But I get it…you wanted to accomplish it on your own."

She nodded, thinking maybe he did understand, after all.

Yet his shoulders remained tense. His jaw tight. Clearly he had more to say. She could see him thinking over how to best express himself.

"I had something else in mind, too, when I bought the place. But I didn't know how to tell you at the time, since I didn't think it was right to mix business with pleasure."

Pleasure?

She frowned, indignation burning away common sense. "You wanted booty-call privileges?"

He looked horrified.

"No, damn it." He stepped closer. Gripped her shoulders. "Alicia, I love you and I want to be a part of this. Help you fix up the place. Realize the dream. I want the chance to convince you that we belong together, and I know I won't have that in Chatham. So I'd like to be wherever you are. If that means taking an apartment in town because you're not ready to move in together—"

Her fingers shushed his mouth, her mind racing to try to take in all that he'd said.

She was nothing short of amazed. She'd had no idea he would entertain such a huge move for her. That he could love her. By God, she had underestimated him— underestimated *herself,* too—because she hadn't considered that he might feel this deeply for her.

"You'd move up here with me?" She'd start with that much, because she couldn't imagine him ditching such a great family—although she understood better than most that Jack would never want to be part of his father's business. The corporate fast track had never been his style.

"I've been waiting for inspiration to figure out what I want to do with my life since getting out of the navy." He reached for a strand of her hair that had blown across her cheek, and smoothed it aside. "I liked the way it felt to be in the service, and now that I'm done, I wouldn't mind finding other ways to serve. Be a part of a community. Help out some neighbors. I like the idea of building a business from the ground up."

"But this isn't some Habitat for Humanity cause, Jack." She didn't want to be another project for him to fix. She wanted nothing less than this man's whole heart. Forever. "I'll pull this off with or without you. I'm more interested in how you feel about me. About us. Can you go back to the part about loving me? Or maybe revisit the bit about how we belong together?"

Had her wishful heart just imagined that? Jack Murphy had never been a demonstrative man. But right now she craved the words. The security. All packaged up with spine-tingling sex with the hottest, most fascinating man she'd ever met.

He took her hands in his and folded them to his heart. Moonlight glinted in his dark brown hair as his shadowed eyes focused intently on her.

"Alicia, I want to be with you always. I felt that way four years ago, but it seemed like too much to lay on you when you were only twenty years old and a junior in college. It wouldn't have been fair to ask you to wait for me when I signed the navy contract, but I needed to be there for Danny. I always knew I'd look you up when I came home. Always."

The declaration took her breath away. And filled her up all over again with visions of what their future together could be like, until she felt light-headed from the sheer perfection.

"Really?" She remembered he'd said something to that effect on the boat, but she'd been too hurt by his long-ago defection to give the statement much credence. "You'd been home for weeks…."

"I didn't want to come on too strong by barreling into your business the moment I set foot in Chatham. And I'd planned on interrogating those old boyfriends of yours to make sure you weren't serious about someone else. I had some groundwork to do." The intensity in his green eyes gave way to something more tender. "But yes, I would have come after you if you hadn't magically appeared in my bed, exactly where I wanted you."

She felt the world shift under her feet, and it didn't have anything to do with the waves rolling over the damp sands. A crevice inside her stitched together, an old wound closing. Slowly, she tipped her head to his chest and absorbed the feel of him by her side.

"Jack, I love you. I've missed you like crazy. The last three days. The four years before that." The leather of his jacket was warm from the heat of his body and she wanted to burrow beneath it to touch him. "If you mean what you said, then I'm holding you hostage here. To-night and every night."

Relinquishing her hands, he wrapped his arms around her shoulders and drew her to him. It was more than an embrace. It was a homecoming.

"I'm going to make you so happy, Ally," he vowed, his breath a soft whisper against her hair.

"Let's go inside and you can make good on that promise sooner rather than later." She found the zipper of his jacket and eased it down to run her hands over the cotton button-down underneath.

"I can do that." His palms roamed over her back, curving around her bottom and lifting her against him. "I can so do that for you."

"I have several sexual favors in mind," she warned him, the cool breeze off the water twining around them. "There's no contest. No bets. Just you serving my every carnal craving until I can't see straight."

Her fingertips slid between the buttons of his shirt and began unfastening. He hoisted her higher against him and carried her up the beach toward the inn, the promise of a future together waiting inside.

"That might not be a contest, but it's definitely a challenge if ever I heard one."

"Good." She grazed her lips over his, savoring the hungry way he nipped at her mouth. "I know you can't possibly walk away from a challenge, so that guarantees a deliciously satisfying night for me."

"Not just a night." He paused on the front porch, meeting her gaze in the dull glow of the wrought-iron lantern perched on a nearby windowsill. "I'm offering nothing less than a lifetime, Ally."

Her heart did a flip in her chest, the words as good as a proposal coming from a man who would never make a promise he didn't intend to keep. Love for him overflowed inside her, a well that had never run dry.

"I know, Jack. And I can't wait."

* * * * *

COMING NEXT MONTH

Available September 27, 2011

You can find more information on upcoming
Harlequin® titles, free excerpts and more at
www.HarlequinInsideRomance.com.

HBCNM0911

REQUEST YOUR FREE BOOKS!
2 FREE NOVELS PLUS 2 FREE GIFTS!

red-hot reads!

*Harlequin Romantic Suspense presents the latest book
in the scorching new KELLEY LEGACY miniseries
from best-loved veteran series author Carla Cassidy*

*Scandal is the name of the game as the Kelley family fights
to preserve their legacy, their hearts...and their lives.*

*Read on for an excerpt from the fourth title
RANCHER UNDER COVER*

*Available October 2011
from Harlequin Romantic Suspense*

"**W**ould you like a drink?" Caitlin asked as she walked
to the minibar in the corner of the room. She felt as if she
needed to chug a beer or two for courage.

"No, thanks. I'm not much of a drinking man," he
replied.

She raised an eyebrow and looked at him curiously as she
poured herself a glass of wine. "A ranch hand who doesn't
enjoy a drink? I think maybe that's a first."

He smiled easily. "There was a six-month period in my
life when I drank too much. I pulled myself out of the bottom of a bottle a little over seven years ago and I've never
looked back."

"That's admirable, to know you have a problem and then
fix it."

Those broad shoulders of his moved up and down in
an easy shrug. "I don't know how admirable it was, all I
knew at the time was that I had a choice to make between
living and dying and I decided living was definitely more
appealing."

She wanted to ask him what had happened preceding
that six-month period that had plunged him into the bottom

of the bottle, but she didn't want to know too much about him. Personal information might produce a false sense of intimacy that she didn't need, didn't want in her life.

"Please, sit down," she said, and gestured him to the table. She had never felt so on edge, so awkward in her life.

"After you," he replied.

She was aware of his gaze intensely focused on her as she rounded the table and sat in the chair, and she wanted to tell him to stop looking at her as if she were a delectable dessert he intended to savor later.

Watch Caitlin and Rhett's sensual saga unfold amidst the shocking, ripped-from-the-headlines drama of the Kelley Legacy miniseries in

RANCHER UNDER COVER

Available October 2011 only from Harlequin Romantic Suspense, wherever books are sold.

Harlequin® Blaze™
red-hot reads

Join us in celebrating 10 years of The Mighty Quinns!

Fan favorite Kate Hoffman brings us her sexy new Quinn heroes, and this time around, they're tracing their roots back to Ireland!

All Quinn males, past and present, know the legend of the first Mighty Quinn. And they've all been warned about the family curse—that the only thing capable of bringing down a Quinn is a woman.

The sexy Irishmen are back in...

The Mighty Quinns: Riley
October 2011

The Mighty Quinns: Danny
November 2011

The Mighty Quinns: Kellan
December 2011

**Available from Harlequin® Blaze™
wherever books are sold.**

www.Harlequin.com

Harlequin Presents®

USA TODAY bestselling author

Carol Marinelli

brings you her new romance

HEART OF THE DESERT

One searing kiss is all it takes for Georgie to know
Sheikh Prince Ibrahim is trouble....

But, trapped in the swirling sands, Georgie finally
surrenders to the brooding rebel prince—yet the
law of his land decrees that she can never
really be his....

Available October 2011.

Available only from Harlequin Presents®.